T0196198

Who's Your Neighbor?

Kelly Phillips

iUniverse, Inc.
New York   Bloomington

Who's Your Neighbor?

This is a work of fiction. All of the characters, names, incidents, organizations, and dialogue in this novel are either the products of the author's imagination or are used fictitiously.

iUniverse books may be ordered through booksellers or by contacting:

iUniverse
1663 Liberty Drive
Bloomington, IN 47403
www.iuniverse.com
1-800-Authors (1-800-288-4677)

Because of the dynamic nature of the Internet, any Web addresses or links contained in this book may have changed since publication and may no longer be valid. The views expressed in this work are solely those of the author and do not necessarily reflect the views of the publisher, and the publisher hereby disclaims any responsibility for them.

ISBN: 978-1-4502-0340-1 (sc)
ISBN: 978-1-4502-0339-5 (ebk)

Printed in the United States of America

iUniverse rev. date: 7/8/2010

*I dedicate this book to my inspirational partner,
Mark Phillips. He listens to my goals and dreams,
and he shares his ambitions and visions with me.*

Acknowledgments

❀

A special thanks to several people who edited, critiqued, and shared their enthusiasm for this book: Mark Phillips, Billie-Jo Stears, Laurel Plagens, Carole McManus, and Beverly Johnson.

Famous Quote

❀

"People have discovered that they can fool the devil; but they can't fool the neighbors."

—Francis Bacon

CHAPTER 1

Tony Henkerson

Tony Henkerson had already tried numerous times to tell his wife that he was leaving and why, but he was unable to complete the task. This letter seemed to be the only way that he could possibly deliver the message without her interrupting him.

He thought that his wife had robbed him of passion years ago, and so he was not surprised that his letter was dull, containing nothing beyond the bare words of plain, non-poetic truth. The last lines were the end of a chapter in his life.

As Tony folded his letter, he gazed at their wedding picture in its beautiful, golden oak frame on top of the glass end table. This was another artifact of marriage that had become a mundane object, like his wedding band: both, grim reminders that something special had once been his and was no more. The ring was a showpiece that alerted the world of his capture, but the picture; it had snagged something, too. He crossed over to it, picked it up, and studied the image of himself: a handsome, young groom dressed in a dark tuxedo holding Robin: a beautiful, young bride in a white, designer gown. It was a dream caught inside of a frame: A time of true love when their hearts were full of passion for one another, and their dreams were delicate and flexible to numerous possibilities of what a life together could mean.

He heard Robin's footsteps in the hallway. Quickly, he set the picture down and stuffed the letter into his back pocket.

"What are you still doing here? You'll be late for work."

"Robin!" He whirled around to face her. "I was just getting ready to leave." He knew he meant that in a much deeper sense. Tony grabbed his keys off the hook on the wall near the kitchen counter. "Bye."

She pulled a tissue from the back pocket of her gray sweats, blew her nose, and wiped it. "Wait a minute. Aren't you forgetting something?" Robin's hazel eyes widened. Her messy hair bun on the top of her head wiggled as she spoke.

A kiss after an argument the night before was out of the ordinary, but he decided to comply. Tony moved up next to her, aligned his face with hers, and puckered his lips.

She turned away, marched into the kitchen, and opened the cabinet door beneath the sink. Robin pulled out the full trash bag. "It's beyond me how you could forget to do something so simple every morning." After dropping her tissue into it, she briskly walked back into the living room and held it out to him. "Well, take it."

"Sorry," he said. With trash bag in tow, he headed out the door.

As soon as she heard him leave, Robin picked up the notebook that Tony had been using, smoothed her hand over the blank page, and felt indentations. She snatched the pencil on top of an unfinished crossword puzzle. Lightly,

Robin ran the lead over the note pad revealing the contents of her husband's letter: Dear Robin, I don't know how this happened to us. I don't know why. I just know it did. I am leaving. Sorry. I want what is best for both of us. Good-bye. Tony.

She moved the curtain open on the front window in the living room and looked down at the parking lot. Her husband was dumping the trash into the dumpster. Fred Greenway, the elderly man from the apartment downstairs, walked out of the building and to his car in the handicapped space. He was carrying a large box that he could barely see over. Robin watched her husband rush over to their neighbor and take the box. She muttered, "You're not going anywhere," and let the curtain close.

As if he could feel her eyes on him, Tony glanced up at the apartment window. He saw the curtain move. Probably checking to make sure I'm taking out the trash, he thought. Don't worry, I'm taking it out, but it will be for the last time. Everything is going to change.

"Thanks, Tony." Fred popped his trunk, and Tony placed the box inside. Fred reached into his pocket and pulled out his wallet. He removed a small stack of bills and held it out to Tony. "Edna and I want you to take this."

"No, I don't want any money."

"We want to give you something for all your help last month when we were away at the hospital."

"What? Watering your plant and collecting your mail? That's not a lot. It was nothing. I was happy to do it. Put your money away. I won't take it. How is Edna?"

"Better. Thank you. I'll let her know you asked about her. That will make her happy. Please, at least let me reimburse you for those groceries you bought us."

"No. I was glad to help. You take care now. I'll see you later." Tony closed Fred's trunk and walked to the apartment door with him. He held the door open.

After Mr. Greenway entered, a blond haired woman exited. Tony continued to hold the door.

"Thank you and good morning." She smiled and walked toward a white Taurus.

"You're welcome. Good morning." He followed her through the parking lot. "I didn't know we had any new tenants."

"I'm not a new tenant. I'm apartment sitting for a friend." She reached for her car door.

Tony walked up to her. "Oh, is it Laura Knight? I haven't seen her lately."

"Yes."

"Is something wrong? Is she all right?"

"Laura's fine. Her mother had hip surgery, and she's helping her, that's all. Bye." She bent down to sit in her driver's seat.

He reached out his hand. "I'm Tony. I'm in apartment 2A, right next door to you."

She straightened and accepted his handshake. "I'm Jill. Nice meeting you."

"Nice meeting you, too. Looks like it will be a nice day."

"Too bad I have to spend it indoors working," she said.

"Same here, but my vacation starts tomorrow."

"Lucky, you," she commented and continued to sit in her car. Jill closed the door and put the window down.

Tony held out a business card. "If you ever need a car, I'm your man."

She eyed the dealership card and accepted it. "Thank you."

"Have a nice day." He smiled.

"You have a nice day, too." Jill started her car and drove away.

As he entered his blue Avenger, a ring tone played loudly. Quickly, he pulled his cell phone from his pocket. Reading the caller ID, Tony smiled. "Sandy, how are you?"

"Excited. You'll be over at eight?"

"Right after work," he promised.

"I love you."

"I love you, too. Bye." He put his phone away and whispered to himself, "I'm going to have a nice day and a nice rest of my life."

CHAPTER 2

Robin Henkerson

Robin was miserable. A month ago, her husband had told her that they were going to vacation separately this year. She complained at the time, but he won out by explaining that a little time away from each other would strengthen their marriage. This worked for her up until last night, when they were both just one day away from starting their vacations. Robin pleaded with him to change his mind, but he was firm in his decision. Angry with him, she had made him sleep on the couch.

This morning, when Robin discovered the indentations of his goodbye letter, she was mad at him for writing such nonsense. After all, he had not given her the letter.

As the morning proceeded, she continued to think about it. A nauseous feeling rose up in her, and she ran to the bathroom. Shaking, hot and now cold, she bent over the toilet bowl and threw up her breakfast. Robin recalled that her last couple of menstrual cycles had been extremely light, and she could not remember the dates. She washed up and then searched through the cabinet under the bathroom sink for a pregnancy test kit.

After utilizing it, she stared at the indicator strip. The realization of the truth slowly set in: She and Tony were going to be parents. The image of a happy family filled her with excitement. Almost running into the kitchen, she picked up the phone and punched in her husband's cell number, but she ended the call before he answered.

His letter sprang to mind. She slowly walked into the living room and looked at the two, large, blue suitcases near the apartment door. Tomorrow, she was supposed to board a plane and go to her mother's home in Tennessee for her vacation. Not anymore, she thought. Her new plans now consisted of saving her marriage, decorating a bedroom for the baby, and preparing herself and Tony to become parents.

Robin pulled the luggage down the hallway, opened the computer room door, and shoved it inside. Things would be different now. As she glanced around the room, she saw the future nursery with a crib replacing the computer, a changing table where the file cabinets were, and a little dresser and toy box next to the empty wall. Lightly massaging her belly, she smiled.

CHAPTER 3

Her Plan

After returning home from the store, Robin pulled out a blue vase from the cabinet above the stove, filled it half way with water, and placed it in the center of the kitchen table. Reaching into one of the grocery bags, she pulled out a beautiful bouquet of red roses and set them into the vase. Admiring the centerpiece, she smiled and gathered her ingredients and utensils.

Soon, the aroma of the apartment was double caramel apple pie. She lit several pretty candles and placed them around the apartment. Then Robin dimmed the lights and turned the stereo to a soft jazz station. She swayed to the music and lightly danced around the living room. Seeing her image in the mirror on the wall, she stopped, examined her hair and clothes, and headed to the bedroom.

Hunting through the closet, she found her knee length, black, rayon and spandex dress. It was low cut and designed to hug her. There was a slit on one side and soft ruffles at the bottom. For jewelry, she chose a quartz necklace and earrings: past gifts from Tony. After putting on a pair of black high heels, she styled her blondish brown hair so that it hung in long, wavy curls. The last touches she added were make-up and perfume, which she seldom wore. Robin gazed at her image in the bathroom mirror, and she thought about Tony smiling at the sight of her. This pleased her until his goodbye letter surfaced again in her memory. While contemplating his affection for her, she heard the phone ring and walked into the kitchen to answer it.

Robin looked at the caller ID. It was her mother-in-law. "Hello."

"Robin, how are you?"

"Well, I'm feeling..."

"Where's Tony? Is he still at work?"

"Yes."

"Will you have him call me when he gets home?"

"Sure. Is there something wrong?"

"The plate on the left is yours."

"What?" Robin asked perplexed.

"Sorry about that. I was talking to Tony's brother."

"His brother?"

"Tim."

"I thought he was in prison."

"They released him early."

Robin thought about his sentence. It was fourteen years. She quickly did the math and calculated seven years.

"He's been here for three weeks now. I would have told you sooner, but you know how Tony feels about him."

"May I talk to him?"

"You want to talk to Tim?"

"Yes."

"Okay." There was a short pause before she called out, "Tim, your brother's wife wants to talk to you."

Robin remembered how much her brother-in-law used to flirt with her and how that always made her husband jealous. She smiled at the thought of a little competition.

"Hello." His voice sounded exactly like her husband's.

"How are you?"

"Good. How are you?" he asked.

"Good. So, you're out early?"

"Yeah. Guess they got sick of me," he laughed.

"Well, it's good you're out."

"I'd love to see you."

"Drop by sometime."

"What about Tony?"

"The two of you should make up."

"You're right."

"Well, it was good hearing your voice again."

"Could I come by tonight?"

"Well," she paused. "We have plans, but a quick visit would be okay. Could you come now?"

"I'm on my way. Bye."

Robin looked at the display screen on the stove. It was eight o'clock. Her husband would be home any minute. With Tim stopping in just long enough to remind Tony about how lucky he was to have her, she did not see how the night could possibly go wrong.

She straightened a couple of the roses on her centerpiece and left the kitchen. Examining the living room, Robin picked up a piece of fuzz from the carpet and headed down the hallway to inspect the bathroom, the computer room, and the bedroom.

Passing the mirror in her bedroom, she noticed that her dress fit a bit too snug. There was a slight baby bump. Before her discovery of the pregnancy, she had thought that her gained weight was fat. For the past three months, she had moped around at work and home, grieving over her father's death, and eating more than usual. It never dawned on her that she could be carrying a baby. She and Tony had not made love in so long that she could hardly remember what it felt like. Strangely, after her father's death, nothing seemed to matter to her anymore, and pleasing her husband was the farthest thing from her mind. Of course, he would want separate vacations. It made sense. No one would want to spend 24/7 for two weeks with someone who was miserable.

Now, things were different. The baby had lifted her veil of depression. All she had to do was convince Tony that she was back to her loving self again, and they could vacation together. Robin thought about how nice it would be if they visited a beautiful, exotic island and stayed in a romantically decorated hotel room that overlooked an ocean.

After fantasizing a bit, she flipped between three television shows, watching them sporadically, read two chapters of a romance novel, and used the battery operated fuzz remover on one of her good sweaters. It was ten o'clock, and Tony still had not arrived home. Just as she was about to phone him again, there was a knock.

Robin wondered why Tony had not used his key. She opened the apartment door and saw her brother-in-law. Except for the big, bushy beard, he looked identical to her husband.

"Look at you!" he said sounding excited. After setting a large, black backpack down in the living room, Tim wrapped his arms around Robin and hugged her in a long embrace.

She pulled away. "It's wonderful to see you. I expected you earlier. I thought maybe you changed your mind and decided not to come."

He laughed. "You know me. I'm never on time for anything." Tim grabbed her again, and this time he gave her a hard kiss on the lips, chafing her skin with his scratchy beard.

Stepping away from him, she said, "I hope you won't mind coming back tomorrow. Tony's not home yet."

"I'll wait." He strode into the living room and took a seat on the couch.

Robin slowly closed the door and followed him. "Would you like something to drink? We have pop, juice, milk, tea, coffee, water," she laughed nervously.

"Does my brother still drink whisky?"

"Yes."

"Whisky would be great."

"Okay. Make yourself comfortable. I'll be right back."

He followed her into the kitchen. "I don't take it on the rocks."

"Okay," she said startled to hear him behind her. Quickly she poured the liquor. "Here you go."

Tim gulped it down. "This place smells like caramel apples."

"Oh, I baked Tony's favorite pie today."

"Could I have a piece?"

"Sure." Robin set a placemat on the table, pulled out a plate and fork, and she cut him a large piece of pie.

Holding his empty glass out to her, he said, "I'll need something to wash it down with."

"It's probably going to be better with milk."

"I never drink that poison. I'll have more whisky."

Reluctantly, she refilled his glass. "I'll be back," she promised. Then Robin walked briskly into the living room and turned off the romantic, jazz music.

"This is delicious," he called out from the kitchen.

"Thank you," she said stepping back into the room.

"I just can't finish it. You gave me such a big slice." He gulped down his whisky and filled his glass again. Tim carried his drink into the living room. "The music was good. You should put it back on."

She followed him. "I want to be able to hear about what you've been up to lately."

He flopped down on the couch. "Prison's kind of a routine, and there's not much to tell."

"No work programs, special interest, activities?" she asked sitting down at the opposite end of the couch.

"I didn't do much of that. Tell me what you've been up to?"

"Oh, just work; mostly typing my life away."

"What about Tony?"

"He's still at the dealership selling cars."

"I got lucky. Mom gave me her old Ford Explorer."

"That's good," she commented and wished that Tony would hurry home.

Their conversation continued to be pleasant for a couple of hours. Then Robin ran out of things to talk about. She looked at the display screen on the television and saw that it was after midnight. "Wow, Tony's really late. I'm not sure what's keeping him. I think I'll try and call him again."

"Is he always this late?"

"No. No. He's usually on time. I don't understand it." Robin thought about the indentations that she had read in the notebook.

"If you were my wife, I'd be home early every night. I'd never be late. Look at this place; look at you." He scooted closer to her on the couch.

She jumped up and walked around the room quickly blowing out the candles. Robin turned the switch on the wall until the lights shone brightly in the living room. "I don't know why I didn't do that earlier."

"I know why you didn't," he said smiling at her.

"I'm worried about Tony. I really don't want you to have to wait any longer. You should come back tomorrow."

Tim walked up beside her and turned the knob on the wall until the lights were dim again. He lit a few of the candles and turned the stereo on. A romantic song was playing softly. "And leave you alone when you're worried? Not a chance. I'm not like that." He rubbed his body up next to hers. "I don't treat women that way," he whispered into her ear.

She quickly left his side and returned to the couch. "You can wait another ten minutes, but after that, you need to go."

He smiled and followed her to the couch. "I love your dress. I love your hair. You're as pretty as I remembered you, and I thought about you everyday." Tim sat beside her and rubbed his leg up next to hers.

As he continued to nudge towards her, she kept moving until she was huddled into the corner of the couch. Now, she was fending off his hands that kept caressing her arms. Gently, she pushed his hand away from hers.

Suddenly, he grasped her left ankle and rubbed his hand slowly up. "Wow, your legs are soft as butter, so smooth." His hand continued up her leg and under her dress.

She smacked him hard on the arm. "Stop! What's the matter with you? I'm your brother's wife."

"You're all dolled up. What do you expect?"

"It's not for you. It's for Tony."

"Why am I over?"

"To visit Tony."

"Tony hates me. I came to visit you." He smiled.

"I hate you, too," she added quickly.

"Then, why did you invite me over?"

"To make my husband jealous. I found out that he's planning to leave me, and I thought that, oh, it doesn't matter. It was a dumb idea."

"I could kiss you when he comes in." He looked across the living room at the apartment door. "That would work." He grabbed her around the waist, pulled her up next to him, and gave her a squeeze.

"No. Just leave. I don't know what I was thinking."

He laughed. "I know what you were thinking." He held her closer and tried to kiss her.

She bit him on his lower lip, drawing blood. "Stop it! Get out!"

Tim raised a fist into the air, waving it over Robin's head. Just as he was about to strike her, the apartment door opened. He saw the shocked look on his brother's face, lowered his arm, and laughed.

Robin pulled away from Tim and stood up. "Thank God, you're home." She saw the puzzled look on Tony's face change to anger. "Your brother stopped in to visit. Where have you been?"

Tony stormed off to the bedroom. Robin ran after him, and Tim followed.

Tony pulled a suitcase out from under the bed and opened the top dresser drawer. He began transferring his clothes to the suitcase.

"What are you doing?" she cried.

"I'm leaving."

"To go on your fishing trip?"

"No, I'm leaving for good."

"You can't." She grabbed his car keys from the top of the dresser.

"Give me one good reason why I should stay."

She was about to yell out that she was pregnant. Instead, she shouted, "Where were you?"

"It doesn't matter. Give me my keys."

Robin threw his keys across the room, and she removed his cell phone from the holder on his belt. "Let's just see who you've been calling lately."

Tony reached out, grasped her hand, and wiggled her fingers lose. "That's none of your damn business." He shoved his cell phone deep into the front pocket of his pants. "Move out of my way. I'm leaving."

"You aren't getting the money in our savings account."

"I don't want it." He pulled his wallet out of his pant pocket and opened it. "Here," he removed all of the bills inside. "You can have this money, too. I just want to leave."

Robin cried and pounded her fists on his shoulders. "You're a monster!"

Tim rushed in, pushed Robin aside, and punched his brother in his face. "Leave her alone."

Tony's wallet dropped on the floor, and he tried to pick it up, but Tim kicked him in his ribs. Quickly, Tony recovered and left the bedroom. Blood dripped from his nose into his open hand.

"Your wife deserves better," Tim yelled, following him.

"You can have her."

"Oh, I can have her? Now that you're done with her, I can have her? I can have your leftovers?" Tim followed his brother into the living room where he hit him again. This time, he punched him hard enough in the head to make him black out for a few seconds and fall into the glass end table, shattering it into pieces with his face.

Robin saw her husband's face bleeding, and she screamed for Tim to leave, but he ignored her. It was as though he was in a trance controlled by his own wild rage.

Tim yelled, "Don't you care about her anymore?"

Robin anxiously awaited her husband's answer. There was no expression on Tony's face. Then she heard him say, "No, I don't," just as though he had been answering about whether he liked cream in his coffee.

She cried loudly, "Tony, I love you."

Tim grabbed Tony up off the living room floor and shoved him into the kitchen where he cruelly beat him while Robin screamed and begged him to stop. She grabbed the blue vase from the table, let the red roses and water spill onto the floor, and threw it at her brother-in-law, but she missed. It crashed into the wall and busted into pieces on the floor.

CHAPTER 4

Noise

It was one in the morning on Saturday. Jill tossed and turned. She put the pillow over her head. Nothing was working to keep the yelling and screaming, the breaking of glass, the slamming of doors from invading her sleep. It was late to be calling a friend, but this was too much. She grabbed her cell phone off the top of the dresser and punched in Laura's phone number.

The voice sounded groggy and deep on the receiving end. "Hello."

"Laura, is that you?"

"Jill?"

"Yeah."

"Is everything all right?"

"I wouldn't call you if everything was all right."

"Is it my cat?"

"No, Laura."

"Is there something wrong with the apartment?"

"No."

"Is..."

"Stop. I didn't call to play a guessing game with you."

"What is it?"

"It's your damn neighbors. They're fighting like wild animals. Why didn't you tell me about this? I would have stayed in a hotel. You did this to me on purpose, didn't you?"

"No. I knew you were getting your house remodeled, and I wanted to help you. It seemed like perfect timing. My mother needs me here, and I needed someone to watch Kittykay."

A loud boom sound came through the wall. "Laura, did you hear that?"

"What?"

"Probably their refrigerator; one of them threw it at the wall."

"That's impossible."

"Whatever! How do you put up with this?"

"It's usually not that bad. They yell at each other. They don't usually throw things. I've never heard them do that before."

"Well, apparently they've run out of things to yell to each other."

"The Henkersons are actually a very pleasant couple when they're not arguing. You know what, there's something in my junk drawer."

"Something in your junk drawer?"

"It can help."

"Is it a dart gun?"

"What?"

"You know, like for wild animals. Something I could tranquilize them with."

"Go to the junk drawer."

"You're talking about in the kitchen, right?"

"Yeah."

Jill got out of bed and hurried into the kitchen. "Which junk drawer?"

"I only have one."

"No offense, but they're all full of junk."

"It's by the stove."

"Okay, I'm at the junk drawer." She pulled the drawer open. "What am I looking for?"

"There's a card in there. Sister Amy from my church gave it to me. It's for marriage counseling. I was supposed to give it to the Henkersons, and I forgot."

"What? A business card? How's this supposed to help?"

"You go give it to them."

"What? Are you out of your damn mind? They're killing each other over there. You want me to knock on their door and say, excuse me. Would you two quit pounding on each other for a second? I want you to read a card!"

"Then, call the police."

"Big help you are."

"Well, I thought it was a good idea. It's one in the morning. I'm half asleep."

"Quit bragging." Jill moved things around inside the drawer. She found the business card and pulled it out. She heard Laura's mom's voice in the background of the phone.

The voice, though low, was clear and sounded panicked. "Laura. Laura. Who are you talking to? Where are you?"

"Mom, I'm in the living room. I'm just on the phone. Everything's fine. Go back to sleep," Laura called out. "Thanks a lot and goodnight."

"Goodnight? Are you trying to be funny?"

After Laura ended the call, Jill returned to the bedroom; placed her cell phone and the business card on the nightstand, and turned off the light. Seconds later, there was a loud purring sound next to her head. She turned on the light. "Kittykay, go sleep in your own room."

The black and white cat stretched and moved down from the pillow. She landed near Jill's neck and shoulders. Playfully she pawed at the collar on Jill's green, cotton pajamas.

Jill picked up Kittykay and carried the cat to her own room where she jumped from her arms and landed on the blue, cushiony pet bed. Agitated, Jill walked into the kitchen and poured herself a glass of water. During the moment that her lips touched the glass, she heard a loud thud and a woman's scream causing her to jump and jerk her glass. Water jumped up and splashed the side of her face. "That's it."

Pulling on Laura's pink housecoat and her own orange slippers, she thought, it is ridiculously late, and I have a right to sleep. With the marriage-counseling card in hand, Jill marched over to the neighbors' apartment. With a bit of righteous indignation, she knocked on the door. When no one answered, she knocked harder.

The apartment door opened a crack. "Who is it?" Tim asked.

"I'm a neighbor. I have something for you." She could only see a bit of his forehead and a few strands of his sandy brown hair as he peered through the opening.

He reached two fingers out and grasped the business card. "Who are you?"

"I told you, a neighbor. Look, I would have called the police, but Laura Knight said I should give you that. She said that you and your wife are a nice couple, and you should go to counseling. You know, some of us have to work in the morning." She took a closer look at the apartment number, 2A, and recalled the man who had held the building door for her yesterday morning. "You're Tony, right?"

A moment of silence occurred before he responded, "Yes."

Jill had expected him to open the door wide and be the gentleman that he had displayed to her before, but he closed the door. Disappointed, she walked back to Laura's apartment.

Tim watched her through the peephole. Then he grabbed Robin's arm and pulled her over to the door. He opened it a crack and shoved her toward it. "Who is she?"

Robin peeked out the door. She only saw the back of the woman. "I don't know. I'll go talk to her." She quickly opened the door and took a step out of the apartment.

He reached out and grabbed her by the neck. "Get back here. Nobody's going anywhere."

Robin gasped in fear. The tightening of his fingers around her throat silenced her cry.

It was the man's harshly whispered words that got Jill's attention. She was about to enter Laura's apartment. Quickly, she looked at apartment 2A and saw the hand around the woman's neck dragging her back into the apartment. Running, she made it to the neighbor's door just in time to have it slammed in her face.

"You let her leave, Tony. You obviously need time to calm down so no one gets hurt. Let your wife leave, or I'm calling the police."

The door opened and Robin quickly stepped out. "I'm fine, really. Thank you for your concern. I'm fine."

"I just saw him grab you. Has he been beating you?"

"No, no, I'm fine."

Jill peered at the woman's hazel eyes and thought she was lying to her. "Did he threaten you? You can stay in my apartment tonight. You don't have to put up with abuse."

"No, I'm fine, really. I'm sorry about all the noise."

Jill looked her over and did not see any cuts or bruises, just some redness around her neck. She wondered why the woman was wearing a dress. She even had high heels on, and her hair was neatly styled. At one in the morning, Jill thought everyone should look as ridiculous as she did wearing a short, pink housecoat over long, green pajamas, and slippers that were orange. Her hair looked like it had hung out of the window of a speeding car. "Knock on my door if you need me. My name's Jill. I'm staying in Laura Knight's apartment for a couple of weeks."

"I'll be fine, but thank you."

"What is your name?"

"Robin, Robin Henkerson."

"Robin, don't be afraid to come over."

"Thank you, Jill."

CHAPTER 5

Identity

Robin lightly tapped on her own apartment door. "She's gone," she whispered.

Tim opened the door. "Hurry, get in here."

She stepped inside, and he closed the door and locked it. Tim stroked his thick beard.

Robin looked at her husband's limp body that was slumped against the kitchen wall. "What are we going to do?" she asked weakly.

He rubbed his big, bushy beard. "I'll shave this, and I'll be Tony. That way neighbors will think he's still alive. You call him off work for a couple weeks. Say he's sick or something."

"He starts his two week vacation today. He was going to go on a fishing trip while I visited my mother."

"Since when has he ever liked fishing?"

She broke into tears. "I don't know."

Tim opened his black backpack. He pulled out a large, black body bag.

Robin gasped. "This wasn't an accident." She recalled Tim entering the apartment with the backpack. "You planned to kill him."

"No, I didn't."

"Why would you bring that?"

He ignored her question. "Get over here and help me out." Tim grabbed his brother under the arms, lifting his body up a bit. "Get the bag open."

"No." She ran to her bedroom and closed the door.

Tim let the body fall back onto the floor. He stared at it for a few seconds and slowly removed the wedding band from the left hand. "Remember, you didn't want to be married anymore." After placing the ring on the kitchen counter, he struggled to get Tony's body into the bag. He then mopped up the blood from the floor, picked up the broken pieces of the end table, and swept up the tiny glass slivers from the picture frame. After a quick glance of the wedding picture, he crumpled it into a ball and threw it away. Then he scrubbed the small amounts of splattered blood off the walls.

When he was finished, he stood at Robin's bedroom door. "Open up."

Robin was on the floor crying and staring at her husband's car keys that were next to her. From this angle, she could see the shadow of Tim's cowboy boots beneath the door.

"Robin, I need you to be a lookout," he said softly. "Just stand by the door and make sure no one sees me leaving."

She picked up Tony's keys and opened the door, seeming relieved. "You're leaving? I'll call the police after you're gone."

"Why?"

"I'll say someone broke in and did this."

"Did what? I've cleaned up the mess. I'm taking Tony's body out of here. I'll be back as soon as I get rid of it. I already told you what we're doing. I'll be Tony for a while. We need time to make things look right between the two of you. If you report him missing tonight, you'll be a prime suspect. That nosey broad would say she knew the two of you had been fighting and that would be the end of you."

Robin walked into the living room and watched Tim drag the big, black bag near the apartment door. Realizing that she still had Tony's car keys in her hand, she walked into the kitchen and placed them on the handmade, wooden key holder. Her mind drifted to the memory when she and Tony had purchased it from a quaint shop on Mackinac Island. Next thing she knew, Tim was standing before her.

"I told you to watch. Get near the door and stay there."

This time she stayed at the doorway as Tim proceeded to drag her husband's body down the stairwell. Thud, thud, thud, it sounded as it hit each step. The zipper caught to the rug and opened. He picked up the junk that fell out of Tony's shirt pocket: a piece of gum, a nickel, and a key, and he shoved them back inside the bag and zipped it again. He flipped the bag over, zipper side up, and proceeded down the steps.

Robin heard the door to the apartment next to hers open just as Tim rounded the corner at the stairs. The noise continued: thud, thud, thud, but he was now out of sight.

Jill asked, "What's going on now?"

"Uh, well, I." She paused. "I threw him out for the night."

"Are you all right?"

"Yes, thank you."

"What's that noise?"

"What noise?"

"A thumping."

"Oh, he took a suitcase with him."

Jill smiled. "Good. Good for you."

"I'm sorry about waking you up again."

"It wasn't you that woke me this time; it was Laura's cat. She was digging her way to China through her litter box."

"I wish I had a cat. Tony's always been allergic to them though."

"Maybe he'll stay gone, and you can get one."

"Yeah," she said sadly. Tears welled up in her eyes.

"I'm sorry. I shouldn't have said that. I hope you two work everything out. Marriage counseling has worked for lots of couples."

Robin cried letting the tears spill down her cheeks. She tried mopping them up with her hands.

"I'm sorry."

Sniffling, Robin put her head down. "I have to go." Just then, Robin saw Jill put an arm out toward her as though she were going to pat her shoulder or maybe give her a comforting hug. She did not want either one, so she quickly stepped back into her apartment and closed the door. Robin looked at the neighbor through the peephole.

Jill dropped her arm by her side. "Goodnight."

It was definitely not that kind of night. It was nowhere close to good, Robin thought as she continued to look through the peephole even after Jill walked away. Moments later, Tim was at the door. He whispered harshly, "Let me in, Robin."

This can't be happening. Please, God, this has to be a nightmare, she thought as she unlocked the door and unwillingly let him enter.

Robin followed him down the hallway. She stood at the open bathroom door and watched her brother-in-law take scissors to his beard, put lathery foam on his face, and then shave it clean. She saw the monster touching and feeling the smoothness of his freshly shaven chin. Now that Tim was beardless, he looked exactly like her husband.

"You can't be my husband. I don't want you."

"I'm not here for you. I'm here for me. And, I'm not going back to prison. Tim's going to die in a truck fire tonight, and the new Tony is here to stay."

Her eyes widened with the knowledge that her nightmarish reality was worse than she imagined. "No, you can't be Tony."

"If you want me to leave, then you treat me like I'm Tony. Once everyone believes that I'm him, I'll leave if you want me to."

"I do. I do," she cried.

"Then call me Tony and treat me like your husband. I'm going off to die now, but I'll be back new and improved," he laughed.

Robin now knew how cold and callous Tim had become since he had been in prison. How could a man kill his own brother and then laugh? She thought about going to the police after Tim left the apartment, but she knew he was right. They would think that she had killed her husband. Even if they did discover that Tim had done it, he would lie and say she was an accomplice. Robin could not chance going to prison, not while she had a baby to protect.

CHAPTER 6

Tim Henkerson

Tim drove his green SUV away from the apartment complex. As he pulled onto the main road, he glanced in the rearview mirror at the bulky, black bag in the cargo area. Hatred stirred in him again. The jealousy was uncontainable. One man's body could only hold so much of it. His perfect brother with the perfect life was gone now. No longer could his mother compare them. How many times had he heard her say, "Why can't you be more like your brother?" He was sure that it was too many. It had happened with grades in school, performances in sports, and simple behaviors around the house. He could remember learning to tie his shoes and his mother bragging about Tony being able to do it so much better.

Tony had everything. He even had a charming way with women. They loved him, and he could have his pick of them. Tim was lucky to have captured the interest of one young lady, Robin. He fell in love and thought the feeling would last forever, but after their third date, she refused to go out with him again. Later, he learned why. She had met his brother and fallen for him. They were married on the very day that a judge sentenced Tim to prison.

When Tim looked in the mirror, he saw failure. He was certain everyone else saw it in him, too. At 28 years old, he was free from the penal system but still imprisoned by the inadequacies he felt. His records stated that he was a rehabilitated person, so why didn't he feel that way?

His first day out of prison, his mother began to pressure him about getting a job. Within a week, he had robbed an ambulance, hoping to find drugs to sell, but had only found medical equipment. Tim had abandoned the vehicle after taking what he could carry. Later, when he surveyed his loot, he was surprised to see a body bag.

Now, he was looking at that very item in the back of his truck and thinking about how it was part of his brother's fate. Without it, he may never have thought about this plan.

After two hours of driving, he arrived at the area he had chosen. He remembered it from his youth, and it seemed like the perfect place: out of the way for travelers, many trees, and not much traffic. A few more feet up, and he would park his SUV for good. As he drove forward, it stalled. He tried to start it up again, but there was nothing beyond a grinding sound.

Tim was about to pop the hood, but then he saw that the gas gauge was on empty. Cursing at himself, he stepped out of the vehicle, kicked the front tire, and ran his fingers roughly through his hair. He cursed, and kicked the tire again before walking to the back of the truck where he picked up an old, blue blanket from the floorboard and covered the black bag with it. Then he locked the doors and walked away.

His plan to prop up his brother behind the wheel and douse the truck with gasoline was ruined. Tim stuck his last cigarette in his mouth and flicked his lighter. Several flicks later, he cursed some more. Even that was out of fluid.

On his walk to a gas station that he remembered driving by, he realized that besides all the small flaws in his plan, there was a major one. A gas station had been built in the same spot where the small bus station used to be several years ago. This presented a problem because that was supposed to be his transportation back to the apartment.

Finally, he reached his destination. Tim read the sign on the front window. The hours of operation were from 7:00 a.m. to 7:00 p.m. He rested, sitting on a tree stump by the edge of the woods.

At 6:30 a.m., the gas station attendant, a man in his sixties, arrived and unlocked the door. Tim crept up behind him and shoved his right index finger into his back. "Go in," he ordered. He moved the man up and down the aisles until he found a shelf with duct tape on it. "Lie down on your stomach and close your eyes." Tim taped his hands together, then his feet, and placed a strip across his mouth. Quickly, he found a gasoline can and filled it. He remembered to grab a couple of lighters. While he was at it, he bagged up three cartons of cigarettes. Then Tim turned his attention to the cash register and pushed several different buttons, but nothing happened.

He hurried over to the attendant, bent down, and tore the duct tape from his mouth causing the man's eyes to fling open. "Keep your eyes shut," Tim shouted. "What's the code to open the register?"

"Hit no sale." The man tried to lift his head up to look at him.

"Keep your head down and your eyes shut. You see me, and you'll be dead."

The attendant lowered his head and tightly closed his eyes. "Please, don't kill me."

"Shut up!"

Tim taped his mouth again, hurried to the register, and hit the no sale button. The empty drawer popped open. He ran back to the attendant and roughly tore the tape from his mouth. "Where's your safe?"

"Back room in the floor."

"What's the combination?"

"31-19-11."

Tim taped his mouth once again and then robbed the safe. Afterwards, he removed the surveillance tape from the video machine. Then he walked away, staying near the tree line just in case someone drove by. Half way to his vehicle, Tim stomped on the tape crushing the plastic into pieces. He picked up the largest part and pulled the tape out winding it into a ball. Then he heaved it far into the woods.

When Tim reached his truck, he poured the can of gasoline into the tank, placed the empty can into the cargo area, and drove away to find another gas station. With his small amount of stolen money, he could afford to fill his tank and the gas can at the next stop. Tim was thinking more carefully now. He placed one lighter into the glove box and the other under the front driver's seat. He had a new plan for tonight, and this one involved Robin.

CHAPTER 7

Reality

Robin heard the apartment door shut, and she awoke startled. "Tony," she called out from the warmth and comfort of their bed. It had to have been an awful nightmare. "Tony," she called out again. No one answered, but she heard footsteps. Quickly, she raced into the living room to see him, to know, to be relieved. There he was, Tony: his light brown hair neatly combed, and his face looked nice and smooth. He was okay, except his blue eyes were filled with frustration. Before she could ask what was wrong, he spoke.

"I ran into some problems. I'll have to get rid of the body tonight, and I need you to follow me."

The horrifying reality set in. It was all real, and she would live out the rest of her days trying to deal with it. Why had she even spoken to him or allowed him inside the apartment? Oh, yes, to make Tony jealous, but he arrived with his own agenda.

"We'll wait until it's dark. I found a gas station that…"

"No, I won't have any part of it," she cried.

"I did this for you."

"No, you didn't."

He gave her a cold stare. "He was hurting you, and I saved you."

"No, he wasn't. You planned to kill him."

"It was an accident."

"Then call the police." She reached for the phone.

"No." He ran to her, grabbed both of her arms, and roughly held them together.

Robin struggled to free herself. "We'll tell the police it was an accident."

"This is what I'll tell them. My sister-in-law invited me over. When I arrived, my brother was dead. She killed him."

"You're lying," she cried and let her body become limp.

He knelt and went to the floor with her. "You know that, and I know that, but that's it for who knows."

"No."

"When you found out that he was leaving you, you were angry, and you lost control and you…"

"Stop! That's not true."

"The only one here with a motive is you. If you want me to leave, then you'd better follow me tonight. When that body's gone, I'll be closer to leaving. As soon as people think that I'm him, I'll go." He released her hands, stood up, and walked into her bedroom. Tim picked up his brother's wallet and money from the floor.

"I have to phone my mother that I'm not going to visit her. She'll be waiting to pick me up from the airport if I don't call her," Robin heard herself say.

"Call her then. Hurry up. I'm hungry." He stepped around her and headed into the kitchen. "Get up off the floor and get moving."

"Maybe I should go see her, so she won't get suspicious."

"No. You need to be with me. You have to teach me to be him. Where's his car keys?"

"On the hook in the kitchen."

Tim took Tony's car keys, and then he placed his truck keys on the hook. "I'll be outside. Hurry up. I want you to show me where he works, where his gym is, if he has one. Does he still work out?"

"Yes."

"I want you to show me where he shops for clothes, groceries, where he rents movies. I want you to show me every little thing about him. Understand?"

When she chose not to answer, he was suddenly towering over her. "Do you understand?" His fist was close to her face, and she saw her husband's wedding ring.

Trying not to cry, she answered quickly, "I do."

"Hurry up with that phone call," he warned. Then he left with Tony's wallet, money, and car keys.

Robin phoned her mother and said that she and Tony had decided to vacation together. She apologized for being so short, but she needed to pack. Robin wanted to tell her mother the truth, and she wanted to call the police, but she knew that Tim was right. She did have a motive.

CHAPTER 8

Sandy

It was a warm, sunny day. Tim leaned up against the apartment building and lit a cigarette. While he enjoyed the pleasant weather, a young, pretty girl with long, wavy, red hair opened her car door, stepped out, and smiled at him as if she knew him. To his surprise, she smiled at him again and continued walking to him in heels that made him notice her long legs. Now, she stopped directly in front of him. He thought, maybe she wanted a cigarette.

She reached up and hugged him. "Oh, my, is this a joke?" she said pulling the cigarette from his mouth. "The nutrition guru, smoking? Please!" She flung the half-smoked cigarette to the cement and stepped on it. "Where did you even get that?" She gave him a big kiss.

"Um, I…"

"You don't smoke."

"I just started."

"Oh, Tony," she said, hugging him again. "You're so funny." She kissed him once more. "I know you thought I'd be late, but surprise, for a change I'm on time. Will you buy me a hot dog?"

"What?"

"I like to eat them at the ballgames."

This is crazy, he thought. My brother was cheating on his wife. "We can't go to the ballgame."

"Why not?"

"Robin and I are going somewhere."

"I thought she went to her mother's."

"She didn't."

"Why not?"

"I don't know." He still couldn't believe it. Tony, you dog, is all he could think.

"What are we going to do?" She frowned.

"I don't know."

"Are you going to tell her?"

"Tell her what?"

"About us. You said that you were going to tell her after she came back from her mother's, but she didn't go. So, you're probably going to tell her now. Right?"

"Yeah," he nodded his head.

"Good. I can't wait any longer. Bo is driving me crazy. He can't get it through his head that we're through."

"Robin's going to be out here any minute."

"Okay. I'll leave." She reached up at him for another kiss.

This time, Tim took charge and gave her a kiss. This is easy he thought. The perks of his new life were already exciting. Her lips felt good, and her body was nice and soft.

She gently stopped their kiss, pulling back a bit. "Tony?" She looked very serious as she stared into his eyes.

Tim panicked. She knows I'm not Tony, he thought.

She continued, "You meant what you said the other night, didn't you?"

"Yes," he answered relieved.

"I've already put my notice in at work. I'm so excited. Aren't you?"

He paused. "I am."

"Are you packed?"

"Getting there," he said, wondering where they would be going. His mother had not mentioned any news about his brother going anywhere.

"It'll be wonderful won't it: you and me and a brand new life?"

This was a surprise. He thought his brother had the perfect life already. "You better go. Robin will be out here any minute." He thought about giving her another kiss, but his own warning words about Robin scared him, also. If his new life was going to work, he needed her help.

"Okay. Tony, but first, I need Bo's house key."

"What?"

"Bo's house key. You had it last night at the hotel."

He had a quick recollection of the items that had fallen from the bag when he was dragging it down the stairs last night. He remembered that one item had been a key. "I lost it."

"Lost it, where? I told Bo I'd give it back to him."

"Bo? Didn't you just say you two were through?"

"We are. That's why I'm giving him back his key. I think if I do, he'll realize I mean it."

"You moved out of his place?"

"Tony, what's the matter with you?"

"I'm sorry. I know you moved out. I'm just worried about Robin coming out here."

"So, let her see us. You have to tell her anyway. You need to do it soon. I'm tired of living in a hotel. Every time you say that you're going to tell her, you don't. You keep moving it back further and further. If I'd known it was going to take you this long, I would have stayed with Bo." She looked sad.

He saw that pout and fell into immediate lust. Quickly, he pulled her toward him and thrust another kiss upon her soft lips.

The apartment building door opened. Tim saw Jill step out. He didn't like the way she was eyeing him in disgust. He remembered her handing the marriage-counseling card to him earlier that morning. She was trouble.

The pretty, redhead let go of Tim, wiggled herself free of his arms, and ran to her car. "Bye, Tony," she called out.

Tim looked at Jill. "That was my sister," he said.

"Yeah, and I'm the Pope."

The apartment door opened again. Robin walked out. "Hi," she practically whispered to Jill.

"Hi." Jill said sympathetically.

"Let's go," Tim called. He made a quick dash for the parking lot, but stopped short of reaching a vehicle since he didn't know which one belonged to his brother. "Come on, Robin," he yelled.

Robin looked at Jill. "Sorry, about last night."

"It's not your fault that your husband's a jerk."

Tim gave Jill a threatening stare. "Hurry up, Robin," he demanded.

Robin looked bewildered. "Excuse me?"

"How do you put up with that?" Jill asked on the way to her car.

Robin put her head down and walked quickly to the driver's side of her husband's blue Avenger. "I need the keys," she said.

Tim followed her. "Go to the other side. I'm driving." He unlocked the doors.

Jill backed her car out of the parking space and drove toward the parking lot exit. At the same time, the redhead pulled her car out in front of Jill's, cutting her off. Jill put her window down, poked her head out, and yelled, "Watch where you're going, sleazebag."

The woman flipped Jill off and spun out onto the street.

Tim and Robin witnessed the near accident. Tim griped, "That nosey, dumb, blond can't drive."

"It was the other woman's fault." Robin shook her head. "She pulled out right in front of her."

"Who cares?"

"I haven't seen her around our complex before."

"Don't worry about it," he shouted.

A few moments later, Robin said, "I see you found Tony's favorite T-shirt. What else did you take of his?"

"There isn't anything of his left. It's all mine now." He watched tears well up in her eyes, and he felt powerful.

They were quiet the rest of the way to the restaurant. During their meal, they didn't talk to each other.

After they finished breakfast, Robin went to the bathroom. When she returned, Tim was examining his brother's wallet. He laid all three of the credit cards on the table and then searched through all of the little pockets. This is when he discovered a rip in one of them. A picture of Tony's girlfriend was inside of the damaged pocket, hidden in its lining. Tim pulled it out and dropped it.

Robin picked it up. "That's the woman from the parking lot. That's the redheaded woman who cut Jill off."

"No, it's not."

"Yes, it is." She held up the picture and turned it over. She read the name, "Sandy," and she looked at the phone number. Now, her attention was on Tim. "You talked to her in the parking lot, didn't you? Did Tony know her?"

"I would have told you, but why hurt your feelings?" He belched.

"You killed my husband!" she snapped. "You're not worried about my feelings!"

Tony yanked the picture back from her. "Keep your voice down."

After paying the bill with one of his brother's credit cards, they quickly walked out of the restaurant. Tim laughed on the way to the car. "He was cheating on you. I told you he didn't like to fish."

She broke down crying. "I thought we were just going through a down time."

"Don't worry. You can divorce me for cheating on you, and then I'll be out of your life." He smiled. "It's perfect, and the neighbors will believe it. That nosey neighbor of ours saw me kissing her, and she knows your husband is a cheating dog," he laughed. Rejoicing in her agony, Tim smiled at her. "I was surprised when she kissed me just like she'd been doing it for years; must have been going on for some time."

"Stop."

He smiled bigger. "So young and so pretty. Hard to believe she fell for him."

"Please stop."

He laughed raucously. "I didn't know Tony had it in him to cheat on you. He has her living in a hotel. That's where he was last night when he didn't come home to you."

"Quit it!"

"Stop yelling." He reached out with an open hand and slammed it into her chest, just missing her belly.

The unexpected strike almost knocked her down. She cried harder.

He got into the car. "Get in," he ordered. "And, stop crying."

She slowly opened the door and sat in the front passenger seat. Robin's crying died down to a sniffle before it stopped completely.

"Where's he work? Is he still pushing paper at that dealership?"

"Yes, I mean no. He's doing the same work, but at a different dealership."

"Tell me how to get there."

"He's on vacation."

"Not forever. Well, I guess he kind of is," he laughed. He looked at her face to see if she caught his joke. She was crying again. He reached out and backhanded her with his right hand, hitting her between her breast and ribs. "I told you to stop crying. Now, tell me how to get to his dealership. I want to go to his gym today, too. I want to know everything about him. Do you understand?"

"I do."

This was all he needed to hear her say. Tim felt confident now. He knew that he had everything under control.

CHAPTER 9

Jill and Laura

Saturday at work had been more trying than usual. Lack of sleep added to Jill's stress. Sitting still in an office and trying to concentrate on paper work without falling asleep had been the most difficult challenge. She was happy to be through with the workday.

It was 5:00 p.m. and cool inside the apartment. The central air was set just right, but there was an odd odor, a stinky one. Kittykay slinked over to her and crawled around her legs. "What's that bad smell? Oh, why am I talking to a cat?"

Jill walked around the apartment until she located the annoyance. Not surprisingly, she found herself standing in front of the cat's litter box. She poured more cat litter into it but noticed no change. Then she heard the apartment door open, and her eyes widened. Jill poked her head out of the cat's room and peered down the hallway to see the door in the living room. Her eyes focused on a head of thick, curly, black hair that looked familiar.

"Just me," Laura said. "I stopped in to pick up a few more clothes. I have to hurry back before she misses me."

Jill walked into the living room. "Must you scare the hell out of me? I know it's your place but knock first."

Kittykay ran to her owner and leapt up. Laura caught her in her arms. "How's my baby?" She hugged her and cradled her. Glancing at Jill, she said, "Sorry, I forgot to knock."

"Try to remember before all my hair turns gray. Hey, let's go out to eat."

"I can't. I promised my mother I'd pick up some Mexican food for dinner. Where's Danny?"

"He's still in Texas. The company isn't doing well in Michigan, but apparently they have money to fly him across the United States."

"That's crazy."

"Ever since he proposed to me, I see him less and less."

"You didn't tell me that he proposed to you." Laura sat down in the chair and petted her cat. "What happened? How did he do it?"

Jill sat on the couch across from her. "There's not really much to tell."

"So, give it to me anyway. Come on, tell me." Her voice and eyes begged to hear the romantic story.

"We were at his apartment. I was taking a bath, and he was watching a football game. His team was winning, and he got excited and just shouted it out, "Will you marry me?""

"He has a television in the bathroom?"

"No."

"So, he asked you to marry him while he was in another room?"

"Yeah."

"Oh."

"Not very romantic, huh?"

"For a Neanderthal it might be."

"Well, it's the first time that any man has ever proposed to me, and I'm in love with Danny, so I really don't mind."

"What if his team had lost?"

"I don't know. I never thought about that."

"When is the wedding?"

"We haven't decided yet. He's been traveling so much lately that we haven't talked about it."

Laura gently put her cat down and stood up. "Well, I better get my clothes before my mother calls. If I'm gone more than five minutes longer than I should be, she calls everyone in my phone book." She headed down the hallway with her cat following behind her. "Whoa, what's that smell?"

Jill yelled from the living room. "Your cat's litter stuff isn't working." She turned on the television.

"You're supposed to clean the poop out of the box. There's a little poop scooper next to it," Laura hollered back.

"Oh. Is that what that is?"

"Are you taking good care of my cat?"

"Yes, of course. I'm watering it, giving it sunshine, and all that sort of thing."

"She's a cat, not a plant. I hope you're petting her and talking to her."

"You know I've never had a pet."

"You promised to take care of her."

"I am. It's just that I'm not good with poop. It smells bad. The idea of playing in a box of it is disgusting."

"What will you do when you have babies?"

"Do they poop in boxes?"

"Come in here, and I'll show you what to do."

"I don't have the energy. Your neighbors kept me up all night."

"Fine, I'll clean it," Laura yelled. She poured the old litter and the liner into a trash bag, and then she put in a new liner and refilled the container with fresh litter. "There you go, Baby," she said softly, petting her cat. "I know you miss me, but Grandma needs me. Just a few more weeks, and I'll be home for good."

Laura carried the trash bag to the apartment door. "See, it's easy."

Jill smiled at her. "Looks like fun, too. Remember to knock before you come back in."

As Laura was walking down the stairs, the garbage bag slipped from her hands and tumbled away. It stopped just before the landing. When she bent down to pick it up, on the step beneath it, she saw a silver key ring with a plastic picture holder attached to it. Inside of the case was a picture of a young woman with long, curly, red hair.

After picking up the object, she continued outside, crossed the parking lot, and tossed her garbage bag of stinky kitty litter into the dumpster. On her way to the manager's office, an old, junky, compact car sped toward her. Its muffler was missing, and the sound was frightening along with its speed and direction. She ran out of its way.

The car skidded into a parking space. A blond haired boy about sixteen stepped out from the passenger side. His hair was at his shoulders. The long bangs fell across one eye. He was tall, hefty, and sloppily dressed. The boy tugged on the waistband of his jeans. The pants rose up and then immediately sagged down when he removed his hand. He hollered to his friend, "Thanks, man." The driver sped off. The boy pulled a key from his pocket and let himself into the apartment building.

Laura recognized him and made a mental note to let Robin Henkerson know that her nephew nearly ran her down in the parking lot. She continued to the manager's office, opened the door, and saw the manager sitting at his desk. "Good afternoon, Mr. Digger."

"Good afternoon."

His hairpiece reminded her of a bird's nest. She tried not to stare at it. "Do we have a place for lost and found items?"

"Sure we do. What is it?"

She held up the key ring.

"Tenants only look for keys and wallets, purses, that sort of thing. No one will come for that."

"I wonder what we should do with it."

"Garbage."

Laura walked back to her apartment still thinking about the key ring in her hand. The mailroom had one mailbox in it for each tenant. It also had two community boards: one cork and one plastic. She picked up the black, dry-erase marker and wrote a message on the plastic board: Lost a key ring? See tenant in apartment 2B. She will be glad to return it to you. Laura felt good; she had done her neighborly deed for the day.

When she reentered her apartment, Jill was asleep on the couch. A talk show was blaring on the television. Laura quietly placed the key ring on the counter in the kitchen. She made up her mind to tell Jill about it later. Laura bent down and petted her cat. Speaking softly, she said, "Now, you behave for Jill. Don't give her a hard time. I love you, Kittykay. I'll be home soon." Without making too much noise, she washed her hands, packed up her clothes, and slipped quietly out of her apartment.

As she closed her door and headed for the entrance, Robin's nephew was exiting from the Henkersons' apartment. Laura stopped him. "Excuse me, Craig? Isn't that your name?"

He walked quickly past her and headed out of the building. "What?"

She chased after him. "Your friend that dropped you off nearly ran me over."

"Oh," he uttered and continued to the parking lot.

"Oh, is all you can say?" she muttered to herself.

She watched him stand out in the parking lot and hold up the keys in his hand. He hit the button on the little keypad. First, he held it up in the air to the left, then to the right. A horn beeped inside of an old, green, four-door SUV. The boy walked over to the vehicle and entered it. It certainly looked like theft to Laura. Even though she had never seen this vehicle in the parking lot before today, it did not seem that it belonged to Craig. After she watched him drive away, her cell phone played a tune. Laura read the caller ID. It was her mother. As she answered the phone, she headed to her car. "Hello, Mom. Yes, I'm on my way."

CHAPTER 10

Craig

Craig and his friend, Todd, attended a couple of graduation parties for friends of theirs. Surprisingly, some of the parents let them drink, and other parents didn't pay any attention to them when they were sneaking up to the bar. At one of the parties, the boys did some pot with a group of strangers who were passing around a large bong. Craig and Todd didn't spend much time at the parties that had heavy adult supervision or didn't serve alcohol. Their graduation party hopping was like trick-or-treat. Each party offered something different.

They were laughing and having a good time. Craig was driving on the highway to the next party when Todd put the window down and yelled, "Stop! There's your ex-girlfriend."

"Let's drink to that," Craig laughed and swerved the SUV to the side of the highway and slammed on the brakes, just missing the rear end of Becky's blue Escort. The girls screamed and ran into the ditch for cover.

"Where'd they go?" Craig asked as he shut off the engine.

"Over there," Todd pointed to the three girls climbing out of the ditch.

The boys got out of the SUV and stumbled over to the girls. "Hey, there," Craig slurred.

"Were you trying to kill us, Craig?" Becky yelled trying to regain her composure.

Craig smiled at her. "What's wrong with your car, Becky?"

She looked at him annoyed. "I don't know what's wrong. Do I look like a mechanic?"

Todd walked a crooked path to the front of the car. "Pop the hood."

Becky did as he asked. Then she and the other girls gathered around Todd. They watched him jiggle some wires under the hood. "Becky, try to start it up now," he called out.

Craig followed Becky to the driver's side of the car. "I want us to get back together," he slurred.

She plopped into the seat, put her foot on the accelerator, and turned the key. Nothing happened. Becky saw that Craig had a cell phone hanging off his belt. "Let me use your phone."

"Why don't you love me anymore?"

"Are you going to let me use your phone or not?"

"Why don't you love me anymore?"

"Look at you. You're drunk. When you're not, you're high. You have no personality."

"I have no person…person..ity. I do, too."

"No, you don't."

"I'll stop drunk." He laughed. "That's funny. I'll stop drunk. I'll stop drunking." He laughed harder. "That sounds so funny."

She held out her hand. "The cell phone."

"No, no, really I mean it. I'll stop drunking." He cracked up laughing. "I did it again."

Craig stood up as straight as he could, and then he fell forward losing his balance. "That's that song, you know, I did, did, did it again." He let out a loud, long laugh. "No, no, I mean it this time. I'll stop drrruu…drrrruu... help me say it right," he demanded, frustrated.

Becky gave him a disappointed look and walked away from him. She rejoined the other girls gathered around Todd at the front of the car.

Todd cleared his voice. "There's something wrong with the engine."

"No kidding, dip wad," Becky's friend, Julie commented.

"You need to be nicer," Todd warned. "We're the ones with the wheels that work."

"Could you get Craig to let me use his cell phone?" Becky asked.

"He doesn't have any minutes on it. Just carries it for looks." Todd explained.

"What an ass." Julie remarked.

Todd slammed down the hood. "That's it." He stumbled back to the truck. "Come on, Craig. Let's go."

Craig stumbled over to Becky and dropped down on his knees. "I promise to quit drunking." He fell on the side of the road laughing. "Ooops, I did it again." Now, he laughed even harder.

"Craig, come on," Todd urged.

Becky stepped over Craig. Then, she turned and bent down, hovering over him. "I'll think about being your girlfriend again if you let me drive your truck," she said.

Craig stopped laughing. "Okay."

The girls returned to the car to get their purses. "Becky, are you going to get back together with Craig?" asked Becky's other friend, Susan.

"No way. I heard from my cousin's friend's friend…"

As Todd and Craig methodically walked a crooked path back to the truck, Craig turned around to see the girls, but they were not following behind them. They were sitting in the car. "What are they doing?" Craig asked.

Todd glanced at them in the car. "Talking. That's what girls do." He now focused his attention on opening the back door of the SUV. "Hey, what's that?"

Craig looked in the back. "I don't know."

"We got to get rid of it and poop up the seats," he laughed. "I mean pop up the seats."

"You said poop up the seats," Craig laughed hard.

"Stop laughing and come help me." Todd opened the hatch and grabbed the blue blanket. He tossed it to the side of the road. He pulled on the black bag. "Craig, get over here."

Craig stumbled over to him. "I feel…I feel…I feel dizzy." He glanced at the bag. "What if it's something im…im…impor..tant?" Craig found a zipper on it and tried to open the bag, but the zipper was stuck.

"Not our problem." Todd lifted one end.

"What if it's something good?" Craig smiled.

"We can come back and check it out later. We'll put it in the ditch. Come on. Get the other end."

Craig grabbed it. "It feels like a body."

"Yeah, right," Todd laughed.

Todd and Craig struggled with the bag, trying to lift it. Finally, they shoved it until it rolled off the truck. Once, it landed on the ground, they kicked it from behind the truck and off the side of the highway. They watched it roll, bounce off a large rock, and roll some more until it landed at the bottom of the ditch.

"Hey, gasoline," Todd said, lifting the can from the back.

"Go put it in the tank."

"All right, and you pop up the seats."

"I'm going to poop them up," Craig laughed.

Todd emptied the gas can and tossed it into the ditch. When he walked up to the cab of the truck, he found Craig on the ground, passed out. "Hey, Becky, come help me."

All three girls helped him pull Craig up. Together, they moved him into the front passenger seat and belted him in. Todd put up the seats in the back, and the two girls hurried inside. He got in the back and sat between them. Becky climbed into the driver's seat. She reached over, slipped her hand into Craig's left, front pant pocket, and pulled out the keys.

As Becky shoved the silver key into the ignition, Craig awoke and put his left hand over hers. "No. You don't. This has to go back to my aunt's. I have to take it back to my aunt's," he slurred.

"Okay."

"You have to take this back to my aunt's."

"You said that already. I've got it."

"You have to take…" His hand slipped off hers, and he passed out again.

Annoyed, Becky huffed loudly. She turned the key, stomped on the gas pedal, and spun the tires, spraying gravel over the blue blanket as she peeled out.

"Todd, which way do I go to Craig's aunt's?"

"Turn around."

"I can't just turn around."

"We do it all the time."

Becky drove off the next exit and crossed the overpass. She entered the highway in the opposite direction. "Todd, pay attention! What's next?"

With many errors and a considerable amount of turning in the wrong direction, they arrived at the Henkersons' apartment. Craig had awakened and unlocked the building door. He guided Todd and the girls into his aunt's apartment.

Becky used the land phone in the kitchen. After calling someone to come and get them, she and her friends helped themselves to cans of pop in the refrigerator and sat in the living room watching television.

Twenty minutes later, Todd walked to the window and looked out at the parking lot. "It's late already. Where's our ride?"

Becky shut off the television. "I don't know. He said he'd come right away."

Craig turned on the stereo and pushed the volume button up. "Let's party!"

Very soon, they heard a pounding sound. Becky opened the door and saw a very upset tall, blond-haired woman.

"What the hell! Are you deaf?"

"Is our music too loud?" Becky asked.

"Is that what you think that is? Turn the noise down, or I'm calling the police. Where is Robin?"

"I don't know. We'll turn it down." She closed the door.

"Craig, turn it down," Becky told him.

"No."

Becky walked over to the stereo, but Craig would not let her touch the buttons. "Craig, move."

"No."

The pounding returned. Todd answered the door. "What do you want?"

"Who are you?" Jill asked.

"Todd."

"Where's Robin?"

"I don't know."

"Turn down your music."

He looked at Becky and Craig fighting over the stereo. "We're trying," he laughed.

"This isn't funny. I was asleep until this noise woke me up. Now, shut it off."

"We're trying."

"Would you like some help?"

"Sure, lady."

Jill stormed into the apartment. Looking at the two teenagers goofing off in front of the stereo, she understood the situation. While the boy was twisting the girl's arms, Jill pushed the power button.

Craig turned and faced Jill. "Huh?"

"What's going on here?" She glanced at the pop cans. "If you kids are drinking pop, why do you boys look so wasted?"

"Who are you?" Craig slurred.

"I'm a neighbor. What are you doing in the Henkersons' apartment?"

"Craig's aunt lives here," Becky said. "We're just waiting for a ride."

A horn honked. Becky glanced out the window to see a van parking. "He's here," she called out. The teenagers grabbed their things and left.

After watching them race out the door, Jill picked up two empty pop cans from the end table and threw them away in the trash container in the kitchen. She noticed a pair of keys on the stove and a key rack above one counter, so she picked the keys up and hung them on one of the hooks. Then Jill locked the apartment door, closed it, and left.

CHAPTER 11

In The Bag

Tony awoke in severe agony. The sharp, piercing, knifelike, stabbing pain was in his head and his chest. The throbbing, dull pain that had developed a rhythm was in his back, arms and one leg. His face even hurt. This far outweighed any pain that he had ever experienced in his lifetime.

It was worse than the time he had hit the diving board with his chest and had broken his ribs or the time when his brother had stabbed a knife into his leg. Even a small twitch of movement caused excruciating torture. It was difficult to breathe. Between the sharp burning and the constant aching, he worried about the body parts he could not feel, like his left arm and right leg.

Go into the light, he thought. Isn't that what I'm supposed to do? Isn't that what people tell you to do when you're dead? If I go into the light, will my pain stop? Will some of my dead relatives' spirits come to take me to the other side? Will my spirit go straight to hell? Which of the Ten Commandments is adultery? What about lying? Wasn't that one, too? I'd done plenty of that, he confessed to himself. Maybe I am dead, and this is hell: you suffer in agonizing pain.

Tony could not see out of his left eye, so he fixed his right eye on the light. You would think the light would be bigger, he thought. Where'd it go? There it is again. He reached his right hand out to touch it. Immediate, sharp pain coursed through his fingers, but he continued to send his hand forward to investigate. While his injured fingers would not bend and grasp as he commanded in his mind for them to do, the skin gave him information: the material felt like leather. I'm alive, he realized. Tony shoved his whole arm forward, sending it through the hole, but after a few moments, he could not breathe too well, and he realized that his arm was cutting off his air supply. Quick as he could, he pulled his arm back into the bag. Cool, brisk air rushed in. As the light came and went, he soon realized it was from headlights on passing vehicles and that it was dark because it was night.

He rested a bit and then tried to move his left arm: Nothing. He tried just to move his left hand. Nothing happened. Tony moved his right arm across his chest and searched for his left arm. There it is. I just have to follow along side it with my right hand. It's, it's, it's under my back and broken at the elbow. I'll just roll over and get it out.

Tony rolled his body to the right a bit, but the left arm dropped farther behind his back. With his right hand, he tried to grab onto it and yank it up, to place it onto the front side of his body, but his fingers would not follow his command to grasp. Now, he realized that his right hand was badly broken and that his left hand and arm were in worse condition. At least he could move his right arm. Tony rolled onto his back again. The pain continued to be excruciating. He cried out, but that hurt, too. Moving his jaw even slightly, sent sharp pain radiating to his ears, neck and head.

After resting a bit, he sent his right hand to finish his devastating and alarming investigation. His only working arm had a hand attached to it that was more like an object in which he had little control over. It served to poke things with and gather only very limited information. At least the skin on it was sensitive to feeling. He shoved it toward his left arm again and discovered that his rolling movement earlier had caused it to flop onto the front of him. There were sharp pieces of bone poking out in unusual places. Clearly, his left arm was broken, and his left hand was in no better condition with mangled fingers in unnatural positions. The fact that the left arm and hand were numb was bad news for his circulatory system. Blood flow was obviously in the danger zone.

He tried moving his toes. The left ones moved inside his shoe, but not the right ones. Legs were next. The left one bent, but not the right. Slowly, he sent his right hand to the questionable area to learn his status. Sliding his hand down, he came to an abnormal bend in his leg. It was worse than he had imagined. His right leg was broken at the shin and trapped under his left leg. He, this time, rolled to the left and all the way over onto his front side. The pain almost caused him to pass out, and now he was covering the hole in the bag. He rolled back over and held his left arm with part of his right arm, pressing his right hand against it, pinning it to the front of him, so to keep it from falling under his back. Now, he was on his back again with his right leg still bent awkwardly. He would have to leave it there.

What happened? I'm all broken up. He slid his right hand up to his neck. It feels straight, he thought. Then, he moved his hand up to his head. It's bleeding. It must be; my hand feels wet. It was too difficult to see his hand inside the bag at night and with only one good eye. The light from the passing vehicles was not enough to be of any help. He returned his hand to his side and used his tongue for further investigation. My tongue moves. I feel the inside of my mouth and my teeth. One tooth is missing from my lower right side. I have to get help for myself or I'll die. "Alp. Alp. Alp ee!" What is wrong with my mouth, my jaw? It's broken, too.

Tony rested his right hand for a few seconds, and then he tried to make the hole larger by shoving his right arm forcibly through the hole, but the material would not give. He thought about kicking his left leg out through the hole, but knowing the position of his right leg, it seemed too risky. After more thought, he searched the inside of the bag with his right hand. He found a zipper. Excited, he again stuck his hand and arm through the hole and flung his right hand on top of the outside zipper, but he could not grasp the little, metal toggle to unzip the bag. His right hand lay flopped on top of the bag like a dead fish. Tony pulled it back inside and let it rest on his belly. In agonizing pain, he lay there, praying for someone to find him.

CHAPTER 12

Robin and Tim

Robin pointed out a few more places to Tim. "That's Tony's barber, and that's where he rents DVD's. That building there is the Moose Lodge. That's where he goes to drink."

"I don't want to know anymore. I'm tired. Just get me some beer and let me sleep." He parked his brother's blue Avenger in a Kroger lot.

Robin hurried into the store. She took a grocery cart and walked up and down the aisles. Am I having cravings? She wondered. Oranges, I have to have oranges and these cheese puff things. She selected enough oranges to fill three plastic bags full. Then she put a variety of snacks into the cart: a bag of cheese puffs; boxes of ice cream: chocolate, vanilla, and strawberry; a bunch of bananas; a quart of strawberries; a container of whipped cream; a bag of pecans; and a jar of cherries. Then, she tossed in a jar of pickles and three cans of tuna fish. On her way to the checkout counter, she walked through an aisle with books and magazines. Scanning them, Robin picked up a publication about expectant mothers. She thumbed through it and began reading an article about what cravings mean.

Tim awoke and went into the store to look for Robin. When he saw her, she was waiting in a long line with a cart full of groceries, and she was reading a magazine. "What are you doing?"

Startled, she jumped a bit and quickly slid the magazine in between a stack of others on the rack. "What?"

"You've been in here for an hour." He glanced into the cart. "Where's my beer?"

He gave her such a hateful look that she realized there were expressions on Tim that she had never seen on Tony. "I'll go get it." She ran off.

As Tim unloaded the groceries from the cart, Robin rushed to the counter with a six-pack of Miller beer. He quickly paid, and they left.

"It couldn't have taken that long to pick out that junk," he griped while weaving in and out of traffic. Speeding and cutting off other drivers, Tim cursed at anyone who got in his way.

By the time that Tim and Robin entered the apartment, they had missed Craig and his friends by ten minutes. Tim placed the bags of groceries on the counter in the kitchen and headed to the bathroom. Robin immediately removed an orange from one of the bags. She washed it and began peeling it.

When Tim finished in the bathroom, he sat down in the living room and turned on the television. He glanced into the kitchen and saw that all of the groceries were still in the bags except for the orange Robin was eating. "I saw ice cream. You better get that in the freezer," he warned.

"Stop ordering me around," she yelled. Robin took her orange and ran off to her bedroom. She slammed the door closed and locked it.

Tim put the groceries away. Then he switched his keys for Tony's keys, exchanging them on the hook in the kitchen. Once again, he sat down in the living room to rest. Before he closed his eyes, he set the alarm on his watch.

Robin had also fallen asleep. An hour later, she awoke and walked past the living room and into the kitchen to prepare a tuna fish sandwich and to get another orange.

Carrying her late night snack, she stopped in the living room and looked at Tim sleeping in the chair. This was the only time that he could ever come close to being Tony, she thought. Quietly, she returned to her bedroom.

Robin sat on her bed and ate. As she swallowed the last bite of her sandwich, she felt the baby kick. A smile spread across her face, and she lightly rubbed her belly. Then, she thought about her situation and began crying. "I'll think of something," she whispered to her unborn child. "Everything will be all right." She picked up the orange and began eating it. "You must like these. I can't seem to get enough of them," she said looking down at her belly.

The alarm on Tim's watch rang at 11:00 p.m. He turned it off and hurried down the hallway to Robin's bedroom. He turned the knob. "Unlock the door."

"Go away."

"You know I need your help. It's dark enough now."

"I can't."

He busted through the doorway, tearing out the framework where the metal lock had once met it. "You're helping me."

Robin backed up in the room, dropped her half-eaten orange, and protectively covered her belly with her arms. "Don't hit me," she cried. She bent her head down and closed her eyes.

Tim stomped on the orange as he advanced toward her. Within seconds, he grabbed both of her wrists in his left hand, and he raised his right hand into the air and swung it across the side of her head, knocking her into the floor.

Robin experienced a few seconds of darkness. There was a ringing sound inside her ears when her sight returned. The disturbing noise disappeared when she raised herself into a sitting position. If he had not been holding her wrists, the force would have sent her tumbling across the room. She saw him raise his hand to hit her again. "Please stop! I'll help! I'll help!" Unable to cover her belly with her arms, because he still held her by both wrists, Robin brought her knees up trying to protect her unborn baby the best that she could. Once again, she tucked her head and closed her eyes, ready to embrace another blow.

When nothing happened, Robin opened her eyes to plead with him. That's when she saw the toe of his black, cowboy boot advancing toward her. Robin twisted herself around, bending her arms unnaturally into a painful position so that his boot grazed her back and her shoulder blades. He released his grip, and she collapsed onto the floor.

"Get up and get your keys. All you have to do is follow me."

Robin stumbled a bit from the dizziness caused by the first blow. As she moved her back, she could feel the damage his kick had done. Sharp pains coursed through her shoulders, arms, back and neck. Painfully, she made her way over to her dresser top where she picked up her purse.

Reluctantly, she followed him out of the building and into the parking lot. Robin unlocked her car and sat in the driver's seat where she waited.

Tim hurried to his SUV, opened the driver door, glanced in the back and saw seats. He slammed the door shut and marched over to the red Sebring. He motioned for Robin to unlock her passenger door.

She lowered the window instead. "What is it?"

Tim reached in and unlocked the door, opened it, and seated himself. "Put the window back up."

She pushed the button. The window closed.

"The body's missing."

"What?"

"The back seats are up. Someone's driven it." He saw a light come on in one of the apartment windows. "Get out. We're going in."

Once inside the apartment, Robin sat on the couch. Tim stood in front of her. "Who drove my truck?" He yelled at her.

"I don't know."

"Robin, my keys were on that hook. Someone had to have taken them, used them, and put them back. Who has a key to this apartment besides you and Tony?"

"Oh, I know." She looked worried now.

He bent down and leaned his face into hers showing her all the frustration lines in his forehead and around his eyes. "Who would take it?" He shouted angrily.

Robin flinched and moved her head back. "I told my nephew last week that he could borrow my car for the night," she said apologetically.

"So, he took my truck?"

"He must have. We used Tony's car, and I forgot my nephew was supposed to come over, so I had my car keys with me in my purse. I was going to take a taxi to the airport to visit my mother, so I didn't need my car, and last week, I told Craig…"

"Shut up! Just shut up. Call him."

"What will I say?"

"Get him over here."

Robin phoned her sister's house, but there was no answer. "They must not be home. They probably went to the police." She hoped.

He ran his fingers roughly through his hair. "Don't say that. I'm trying to think."

"What will we say when the police get here? If we tell them that it was an accident, maybe it will all be all right."

"I told you to stop. Don't what if." He knelt down in front of her and grabbed her chin, pulled it up, and forced her to make eye contact with him. "Let's say you're right. The police know. Here's what you will tell them: Your husband, me, Tony, accidentally killed his brother, Tim, in self-defense." He gave her a long, threatening stare. "You will say that."

She nodded her head. A tear made its way out of her right eye.

"I want to hear you promise. Tell me you'll say it."

"I'll say it," she cried. Suddenly, she felt nauseous and stood up. "I don't feel well. Let me go to the bathroom."

He stood up and blocked her. Reaching for her arms, he noticed they were swollen and beginning to bruise. "Put a sweater on or something with sleeves." Tim stepped back, and Robin quickly ran down the hallway. He sat down in the recliner and wrung his hands repeatedly, waiting.

Knock. Knock. Knock. The knocks were loud and insistent.

Jumping to his feet, Tim rushed to the door. Before opening it, he peeked through the peephole. His shoulders relaxed, and he took a deep breath and let it out slowly. He turned and glanced down the hallway to see Robin walking out of the bathroom. Pointing to the bedroom, he whispered harshly, "The sweater." Tim waited for her to exit the hallway. Then he swung the apartment door open and gave Jill a big frown to display his disgust. "Hello."

Jill ignored his disposition. "Is Robin home?"

"Robin," he shouted toward the bedroom. "She'll be here," he said, leaving Jill standing just outside the doorway.

He sat on the couch in the living room and focused on the TV.

She searched through her closet and could only find a thick, wool sweater. Quickly, Robin donned it and hurried into the living room. "Come in," she urged, motioning Jill into the apartment.

Jill took only one-step inside. "I know it's late, but I…"

Tim grumbled, "Yeah, it's frickin 11:30. Who the hell visits…"

"Sorry, but I heard a lot of shouting, so I knew you were awake."

Tim glowered at her. "What do you want?"

"There were some teenagers in your apartment earlier."

He stood up, pointed the controller at the television, and shoved his finger down on the power button. The screen went black. "Come all the way in. We don't bite," he forced a laugh. "Who was in here?" he asked anxiously.

Robin moved closer to Jill, reached out, and took hold of her closest arm. She gently pulled her farther into the apartment. "Come in and sit down," Robin coaxed as she guided Jill over to a chair in the living room.

Jill sat stiffly in the chair. Robin remained standing next to her.

Tim again sat down on the couch. He began grilling Jill. "Who were they?"

"They told me that Robin was the one boy's aunt."

"How many were there?" Tim asked.

"Five, six. No, it was five. Two were boys and the rest were girls."

"What were they doing?"

"I think the boys were drunk. Their breath smelled like they'd been drinking, and they were acting strange. The girls were drinking pop. They were listening to music, extremely loud music."

"That's what they were doing? What about the truck? Did they come here in a truck?"

"I don't know what they drove. I'd been sleeping, and their racket woke me up. I came over here to make them turn it down. Well, that's everything." She stood up to leave.

He shot up off the couch. "Wait," he practically yelled at her.

Jill froze. Her eyes widened.

"How did they leave?" he asked.

"I don't know that either. Look, I have to go." She quickly walked around him and hurried to the door.

Robin raced after her and grabbed the knob before she did. "Thanks for letting us know about this." Then she saw Jill staring at her back, trying to see something.

"Your tag is out. I'll get it for you."

"No, that's okay," Robin protested, but it was too late; she could feel Jill pulling the back of her sweater gently away from her neck and tucking in the tag. Robin heard her softly utter a gasp of shock, and she knew that Jill had seen the injury.

"Bye." After closing the door, Robin looked at Tim to see if he knew what had just taken place.

He was staring out the window. "We need that nephew of yours," he grumbled.

"Do you want me to phone my sister again?" Robin asked. She sounded tired and confused.

"No. We're going to drive over to your sister's, sit in the driveway, and wait for your nephew. That's what we're going to do."

CHAPTER 13

Bo and Sandy

Saturday night, at 11:30 p.m., Sandy heard someone knocking on the door. She crept out of bed, crossed the hotel room, and peered out the peephole. "Who is it?" She gathered her white, silky nightgown together in the front of her and opened the door slowly, peering down the hallway.

Bo stepped around the corner. "Hello, Sandy."

"Go away," she yelled, trying to close the door.

He quickly shoved the weight of his body up against the door, and with a slight push, his muscular physique opened it wider. Bo pushed his way past her and into the room.

"Come home."

"No. How did you find me?"

"Your sister told me. Now, come home."

"No."

"Whatever it is, I can fix it. Just come home."

"No, you can't fix it."

"Talk to me, Sandy. Give me a chance."

"I've fallen in love with someone else." She read the hurt look on his face. "These things just happen."

Bo flexed his muscles in the mirror as he walked by it. He pulled her up against him. "I love you."

His arms felt like hard objects and this made her think about Tony's arms that were comforting and snuggly. Somehow, Bo always managed to look at his image. No matter where they were, he could find a mirror. He never looked into her eyes and into her very being the way that Tony did.

"You don't even know me," she said.

"What? We've known each other since we were ten. That's, let's see, eight years."

"It's not how long you've known me that makes you know who I am. It's something else."

"You're not making any sense. What makes me know you if it's not me knowing you?"

The word magic came to her mind. With Tony, that is what it had been. The first time they met, it was like he had known her his whole life. They met last year at the fitness club. She was sitting in the lobby reading a book while she waited for Bo to finish his six-hour work out session. Tony sat down across from her and opened a book. She wondered what he was reading. "Hi," was all he had said to her, but it was how he said it. The eye contact had feeling in it, sincerity. "Waiting for the significant other?"

His smile had been her new day. With it, he had changed her boring, humdrum schedule: attend college, do homework, clean the apartment, go to the fitness center, work out for an hour and wait for Bo. That day, Tony had been right; she was waiting for her significant other, and now he had arrived.

"My wife is getting her hair done. It'll take the stylist hours to create this nest thing that you women like to wear to weddings and proms," he chuckled. "What are you reading?"

"It's just something for college. What are you reading?" she asked.

"Oh, it's a fantasy book, my portal to another world, one that's fun."

He was looking for the same thing: fun. Already, they had so much in common. "Those nest things you talked about, they take a long time. My guy's a body builder. That takes a long time, too."

"I take it you spend a lot of time here together?"

"Yes and no. We spend time here but not together. His regiment is too strenuous for me, and he won't compromise any of his routine to spend a moment relaxing with me. I like to work out but in a relaxing way. You know, swim, some light yoga, maybe a little tennis."

"Right. Work out without your body catching on."

"Exactly." She smiled.

"I play a little tennis, but I don't have my racket on me." He smiled.

"We could swim."

He peered past her and saw his wife in a chair at the shampoo bowl. "My swimsuit is in my locker."

They went swimming that day. A week later, they met for a tennis game. This led to movies and dinner.

"What?" Bo demanded to know.

Sandy focused on the moment. "Interests: We don't do anything together that we both like. We don't even like the same movies, food; you name it. We're like day and night."

"Those go together. They need each other."

"It's not that simple."

"Sandy, you can't leave me; the competition's next week. How am I going to win if I'm stressed out?"

"Why is it always about you?"

"It's not."

"Bo, we're through. I told you that. Now, you need to leave me alone."

"Who is the guy?"

"It doesn't matter who he is. You and I are over."

"I know who he is. He's that guy you said was your cousin. He's not your cousin is he?"

She had only been seeing Tony for one month when Bo found Tony's phone number on her cell phone; his e-mail on her computer; and a mysterious man walking her to her car at the mall parking lot. Since the e-mails had been nothing more than conversations for arrangements to meet for nonromantic activities and the walk to her car did not involve tactile contact, a cousin was a good explanation. She knew Bo was extremely jealous.

"Bo, it doesn't matter who the guy is. I don't want to be with you anymore."

"He's not your cousin is he?"

"What does that matter?"

"You've been cheating on me."

"Not exactly."

"What does that mean?"

"He's someone I see for..." She almost said fun. "Therapy," she chose to say.

"He's a shrink?"

"No."

"What is he?"

Sandy wished she had an answer that would save Tony from Bo's wrath. "He's a friend."

"You've been cheating."

"No, I haven't. I broke up with you, so I could have a new relationship. I never had sex with him while I was with you."

He gave her a hurt look. "I want you back."

"No. You're a narcissist."

"What is that?"

"It means you love yourself."

"No, I love you."

"All you care about is your body and your competitions. I want someone who cares about me."

"I told you I do care about you. Would I be here if I didn't?"

"Yes, you would. Remember, you're here because you can't afford to be stressed out before your competition."

"Sandy, I love you."

"Name one thing that we do together that I like to do."

"That's easy," he said rubbing his body up against her.

"Besides sex."

He paused uncomfortably. "We um…We like to do stuff together."

"What stuff?"

"He lives in the same apartments my friend Derrik does."

"Why aren't you naming something that we both like to do?"

"Derrik saw you at the tennis courts, just outside his apartment. He told me that he thought you were cheating on me. I told him it wasn't like that; you were cousins." Bo pounded his fist together. "You both made a fool of me. He's going to pay for this," Bo warned as he stormed out of the hotel room.

"You leave him alone, Bo," Sandy yelled, half warning him and half pleading with him. Sandy quickly unplugged her cell phone from the nightstand and punched in Tony's number. She waited in desperation for him to answer, but he did not. After waiting a considerable amount of time, she phoned again and waited even longer. Still, he did not answer. Panicking, she dressed, grabbed her purse, and hurried to her car.

CHAPTER 14

Flies

Lights from passing vehicles shone near Tony and intermittently broke up the darkness. His head felt heavy as he raised it up and placed his good eye next to the hole in the bag. Holding it there for a couple of seconds exhausted him. Hopelessly, he lowered his head. A couple flies buzzed near his face. One landed on Tony's forehead and crawled across the skin between his eyes. It stopped just before his nose, staying still, so that he could see its dark silhouette.

The energy Tony used to lift his head drained his strength and increased the already excruciating pain in his jaw and ribs. Realizing now that he had no memory about someone putting him inside this bag, he surmised that he had been unconscious. How long? He wondered. Could I be starving to death? Am I dying from dehydration? How long can my body go without food or water? Placing his right hand through the hole in the bag, he moved it over the zipper again, wishing he could control his fingers. With no better luck than before, he retrieved his hand to his chest.

If only my pain would stop, perhaps I could rest and get up the strength to escape this bag. If I could just drag myself to where the traffic is, someone might be able to see me, he thought.

Sleep, sleep, sleep, he begged his mind. What if I am asleep already? What if this is a nightmare? Then, I just have to wake up. No. No, it can't be. Nightmares are scary, but there's no pain involved. This is real. I'm dying along the roadside. I'm as good as dead. Well, not yet. As good as dead: now, I know why they say that. It would be good to be dead. I'd be out of this terrible pain, or would I? How do I know? What if I die, and the pain doesn't stop? Oh, that would be hell. What is hell? It's that place full of fire and brimstone, but what if it's not? What if there is life after death? No, no, what if there is reincarnation? I could come back as a spider and spin a huge web to catch all these damn flies buzzing all over my face and in my ear.

The flies were extraordinarily loud, more so than they were earlier. He could actually feel them buzzing near his right, broken leg. That's good, he thought, I can still feel sensations. Then, he wondered how the flies could buzz enough to cause vibration. Suddenly, he knew that the vibration was not flies buzzing, but a cell phone vibrating. As carefully as he could, so as not to generate more pain, he sent his right hand into his right pocket to retrieve it. His hand found the hard, plastic object, and he was able to maneuver his hand enough to get the cell phone out of his pocket. He held it in between his wrist and torso, managing to slide it up over his broken ribs. This caused more pain. Warm tears slid down the side of his nose and touched his upper lip. As he reached with his tongue to lick the tears and trick his thirst, a severely sharp pain shot through his jaw and radiated for a few long moments causing him to groan in anguish. The buzzing stopped. He lowered his hand to rest. How much pain can a human being handle? I thought incredible pain made people pass out. Why hasn't that happened to me?

When some strength had returned to him, he pulled the phone directly in front of his face and used his right hand to press the keypad against his nose. He pushed a nine button with his nose, then a one and another one. Surprised that he was able to use his nose to accomplish this task, he wondered why it was not broke. I must have fought with someone. How could so much of me be broken and somehow not my nose? Maybe it is broke, but it's numb.

"Nine one one. What's your emergency?"

"I...in a...ag. I in...jur."

"What are you saying? I can't understand you?"

"I...in...jur. I...in...a...ith. I...in...ag. I nee...hel."

"Sir, please speak clearly. Where are you?"

"I dugh naugh. I...ay. Near i...ay." Each word generated new pain, this time in his ribs.

"Where?"

"I dugh naugh."

"Where do you live, and what is your name?"

"I dugh naugh. Ed urts." He touched his head. "Ed urts. Eeding. It eeding. El ee. El ee. Eee el."

"Sir, how are we supposed to help you when we can't understand you?"

He stopped trying to talk. The operator said something about him not being on a landline, and she would not be sending an emergency vehicle to him. Tony shoved the phone into his nose and pressed the end button. It had taken too much energy to punch the three numbers with his nose the first time. Tony focused his right eye on the lit keypad. There was a button marked friends and relatives. He pushed the button and read several names and titles. Mom, number three, stood out. He pushed number three with his nose.

It rang for a bit, and then a woman's voice answered, "Hello."

"Ah."

"Who is this?" She looked at her caller ID. "Tony?"

"Ah."

"Tony? You don't sound well."

"Aaah. I i ah ith i a ag. I ay." As he continued to repeat this, his pain increased until what he had wished for earlier, finally happened: He passed out. Not now, was his last thought, as the blackness and silence overtook him.

"Tony? What's going on? Tony, I think we have a bad connection. I'm going to hang up and call you back. Bye."

The buzzing and vibrating of the phone, moments later, did not alert Tony. His mind and body were no longer consciously aware of anything.

CHAPTER 15

Strange Uncle Tony

Just after Tim parked his SUV across the street from Craig's home, Robin's cell phone began playing music. She looked at the caller ID. "It's your mother."

"Don't answer it."

"It's past midnight. It must be something important. She would never call this late if it wasn't. We should answer it."

"No!"

Robin let the music play until it stopped. A minute later, the music played again for a few seconds. "She left a message." Robin hit the button and listened. "Oh! Thank God!" she said excited.

"What is it?"

"He's alive!"

"Who's alive?"

"Your mother said that Tony called her. The connection was bad or something. She couldn't make out anything that he said. She's worried that something is wrong. She thinks that something must be wrong because he called her so late."

"That's impossible. Someone's playing games."

"Oh." Robin said, disappointed. Then with more contemplation, it occurred to her that Tim could be wrong. She remembered that when she was arguing with Tony, he had shoved his cell phone down into his front pocket. "She said that she knew it was his voice but couldn't understand the words. Who could have called her from Tony's phone and sounded like him?"

"I don't know, but I know Tony's dead. He didn't make that phone call."

Robin wished Tony were alive. If he were, she could tell him about their baby. She wondered how excited her mother-in-law would have been to know the news. Lately, whenever she and Tony visited her, she always wanted to know when they were going to make her a grandmother. She closed her eyes, remembering the happy times and pleasant conversations that she and Tony used to have about their future of parenting. They had gone as far as to select names. She smiled with that memory in her mind and then drifted off to sleep.

A half an hour later, a van drove up and stopped in front of the house, and someone jumped out and slammed the door shut. The van sped off. The silhouette weaved from side to side and then stumbled to the porch of the house.

"Robin, wake up." Tim grabbed her shoulder and shook her awake. "Is that him?"

She looked at the silhouette that was grabbing its pants and pulling them up at the waistband. "Yes."

Tim quickly left the truck and ran after him. Just before the boy unlocked the front door, Tim grabbed his shoulders. "Craig?"

"Hey, man, let me go."

"Aunt Robin wants to talk to you."

Craig relaxed. "Oh, Uncle Tony."

He removed his hands. "She's in the truck." Tim headed to the truck and looked back to make sure that the teen was following him.

Craig had not moved. He stood weaving a bit. Tim stepped back, grabbed onto Craig's right shirtsleeve, and guided him to the truck. He opened the back door on the driver's side. "Get in." He heaved the teen into the truck and climbed in beside him.

"What's up?" Craig asked.

Tim leaned forward, "Robin, drive."

"Where?"

"The apartment." He stayed leaning forward until she started the truck and backed out of the driveway. Tim sat back in his seat, turned to Craig, and leaned into him. "Borrowed this truck, huh?"

"What?"

"The truck, stupid."

When Craig didn't answer, Robin whispered to Tim. "Uncle Tony doesn't call his nephew stupid."

Tim cleared his throat. "I'm just playing, Craig. You're not stupid."

"Aunt Robin said I could use her car, but I couldn't find the keys. So, yeah, I borrowed it."

"Do you remember something being in it?"

"Um, well, I was a bit wasted."

"You're still a bit wasted," Tim informed. "Do you remember a bag?"

"Oh yeah."

"Do you know what was in it?"

"No."

"Where's it at?"

"In a ditch."

"Where?"

"By a road."

"What road?"

"75."

"That's a highway."

"Yeah."

"Where at on the highway?" Tim was letting the anger in his voice come out.

"Becky's car broke down. We gave her and her friends a ride. We needed seats for them, so we had to dump that bag."

"Where the hell did you dump it, shit head?"

Craig's eyes widened, and Robin shook her head. "Uncle Tony is always nice to his nephew," she reminded Tim.

"Answer me, Craig," he demanded.

"In a ditch. What was in it?"

"That's not your damn business. Where's the ditch?"

"75."

"Where at on 75?"

"Near Becky's car."

"Tell your aunt how to get to that car."

"I was messed up. I don't know where on the highway we were at." Craig answered, sounding scared.

"Calm down, Craig. Nothing is going to happen to you. Robin, drive to the apartment. Get your car and follow me." He put his hand on Craig's shoulder. "You're staying with us until we get that bag."

"But, Uncle Tony, I don't know where it is. I can't remember where we were on the highway."

"Sure you can, and you will."

Robin knew that her nephew was afraid. She could hear it in his voice. The last thing that she wanted to do was to involve her sister's son in her nightmare.

CHAPTER 16

More Noise

Dressed in silky, white fabric, Jill lay on a beautiful, soft leather recliner near the shoreline of the ocean. The tropical breeze gently caressed her body with a relaxing motion that felt like a heavenly massage. Mr. October, the male model from Laura's calendar, the one that hung on her computer room wall, suddenly appeared before her. His muscular, tan body dressed in skimpy, red swim trunks made her quiver. In a deep, sexy voice, he asked, "May I rub a little of this coconut oil into your skin?" He smiled. His perfect, white teeth glistened in the sun.

"What are you waiting for?" she uttered. Without hesitation, she slid over on the recliner. It morphed into a king sized bed, and he sat down beside her. His dark, wavy hair bounced in slow motion as the gentle wind played with it. His smooth, flawless skin was touching hers. Now, he was beside her, wearing nothing but her white, silky sheets. The ocean's waves teasingly splashed up to the shoreline near them. Jill and her dream lover playfully swished their feet into the warm water. He smiled handsomely, and she lightly giggled. Then he took her in his powerful, yet gentle arms and thrust a deep, passionate kiss on her hungry lips. Beautiful music began to play, and millions of floating candles speckled the ocean. Mr. October glided his hands tenderly over Jill's body, massaging her neck, shoulders, and her back. His sensual, caressing movements relaxed her mind and awakened her skin. Every inch of her belonged to him, and as he reached beneath the sheets, heightening her anticipation, a buzzer sounded. It was loud and annoying. Where was this intrusion coming from? Neither of them could see what made this racket. The sunset vanished, the ocean disappeared, and the sandy shore dissolved into nothingness. Jill turned toward Mr. October only to see his eyes dull and his face and body fade away.

The tropical trees turned into walls that surrounded her. In this new setting, there were three podiums and a huge lit game board with prizes painted on it. Jill was a contestant. The game show host was Bob Barker. He shouted out, "Push your buzzer when you want the wheel to stop. Where ever it stops, you win that prize." Buzz, buzz, buzz. Jill kept pushing the huge, rubbery, orange button in front of her. She was trying to win the new car, the million dollars, or the plasma screen. Buzz. Buzz. Buuuzzzz. Buuuzzzz. The host announced, "Push your buzzer first, and you win all the prizes." She pushed and pushed, but her button suddenly stopped making sounds. "You lose," he announced, laughing.

Bo gave up on that tenant and pushed some of the other buttons. Someone had to be awake.

Fred Greenway heard the buzzer. He looked over at Edna who had finally fallen asleep after a great deal of difficulty with pain. Quick as he could, he made it to the kitchen and pushed the intercom button.

"I need to talk to Tony Henkerson."

"Who are you?"

He paused for a moment. "I'm his cousin."

"Have Tony buzz you in."

"His buzzer's broke."

Fred heard Edna stir in her bed. Quickly, Fred pushed the button and buzzed the visitor in. He returned to the bedroom to find Edna awake and in pain. She had the bottle of OxyContin in her hand. Fred gently worked it out of her clutching fist. "No, Sweetheart. You can't have anymore until six hours. Try to go back to sleep." He rubbed her back softly.

Bo rushed into the building and headed straight for the mailroom. Reading the mailboxes and apartment numbers, he soon had what he needed. He climbed the stairs and pounded on apartment door 2A.

Pound, pound, pound: the rude noise made its way into Jill's head, knocking her dreams out of the way, hitting her raw nerves. Automatically, her eyes flung open. She looked at her alarm clock. It was one-thirty in the morning. Jill sat up and listened. The racket was coming from next door. Jill put on her housecoat and walked to the apartment door. She peered out the peephole but did not see anything. She unlatched the lock, opened the door, and looked down the hall at the Henkersons' apartment to where a large, muscular man was beating his fist against their door. The quick, sudden turn he made, frightened her. His face was very angry looking. Quickly, she backed up and shut the door. Not sure what to do, she hesitantly stood there. Seconds later, Jill heard him marching down the hallway. The building door slammed.

Moving the curtains aside in the living room, she looked out at the parking lot and under the dim lights of the lamppost. She saw him enter his car and slam the door. Another car pulled up beside his. A woman sprang out, ran to his car door, and knocked on the window. She yelled something at him. Jill quietly pushed the window open, so that she could hear her words.

"Tony didn't do anything wrong. You leave him alone. Bo, you leave him alone."

Jill recognized her. It was the redheaded, young woman who she had seen kissing Tony in front of the apartment building.

Moments later, Jill saw an SUV pull into one of the Henkersons' parking spaces. Robin stepped out and started walking over to her car. Tony exited from the back passenger's side, walked around the truck, and reentered it on the front driver's side. Someone else inside the vehicle climbed from the back up to the front passenger seat. The redheaded girl ran from her car to Tony, and the man with the muscles bolted from his car toward the truck. The girl tried to get in between him and the truck, but he simply shoved her aside and opened the driver door.

Jill watched the man fling the door open and grab Tony by the collar. He yanked him out and punched him in the head. The girl screamed for him to stop. Robin had just opened her car door. Now, she shut it and ran back to the truck.

Smiling, Jill opened the curtain wider. "Serves him right," she whispered.

"Bo, stop!" The young girl screamed.

More people began turning on their lights and looking out their windows. Tim glanced at the audience and then back at Bo. "If you're here for that key, I don't know where it is."

"I'm not here for a key. My girlfriend has it in her head that she's running off with you. I told her I'd kill you first," Bo shouted.

"Go ahead then," Tim dared.

Bo threw a punch to his face. Tim tried to duck, but Bo's fist caught him in the left eye. Tim punched back with a right hook to Bo's jaw and a left jab to Bo's abdomen. He kneed him in the groin, and Bo fell to the cement.

Sandy hugged Tim. "Tony, I'm so sorry."

Robin stared at her. "Get away from him."

Tim removed Sandy's arms from around his waist. "I don't want anything to do with you anymore. Leave me alone," he shouted.

"Tony," she pleaded and hugged onto him again.

"I mean it. Stay away from me," he shouted louder, shoving her away.

Robin walked up to the girl. She had her hands balled up into fists.

Tim yelled to her. "Go get in your car!" He held his hand over his injured eye and climbed into the passenger side of the truck. "Craig, scoot over. You're driving."

Craig climbed into the driver's seat. "Oh, okay, Uncle Tony."

Robin stood there looking at the girl who was younger than she was by at least ten years. Her shirt and shorts were revealing a firm, shapely body, and her long, red, curly hair framed a beautiful face. "You were sleeping with my husband," Robin called out accusingly.

"No. Well, a little." She answered with no remorse.

"Get in your car," Tim yelled again. He looked up at the lit windows of the apartment building where he saw Jill standing at her window with a phone to her ear. "Go, Robin, before someone calls the police."

As though she had broken from a trance, Robin moved quickly to her car. As the truck pulled away from the parking lot, she followed it.

Tim's eye was already swelling, making his sight blurry. The truck was weaving on the freeway. "Keep it on the road, Craig."

"I'm tired. I think I'm going to fall asleep, Uncle Tony."

"Are we close?"

"Close to what?" he asked yawning.

"The bag," he shouted.

"I don't know."

Tim spotted a 24 hour diner. "Pull over into that food joint. I'm going to pour some coffee into you."

CHAPTER 17

Highway Patrol

At 2:00 a.m., on Sunday, Officer Dobbs and Officer Hall were patrolling the highways when they came across an abandoned, blue Escort. Officer Dobbs turned on the police lights, pulled over, and parked behind the car. He accidentally hit the siren. It played for a few seconds.

Tony heard it and pulled his head up, placing his good eye next to the hole in the bag. He saw the lights and tried to yell, but his broken jaw prevented him from doing so. My cell phone, he thought. I have my cell phone. Tony used his wrist and arm to, again, shove the phone up to his face and press the keypad into his nose. He hit the volume button repeatedly until it was up all the way. Now, I just need to push the button to test my ring tone, he thought. If I can find that button, my phone will play music for a few seconds at least. Maybe by the grace of God, whoever has stopped on the side of the road will find me. He was in excruciating pain as he tried to push the correct button. No, please, no, he pleaded with himself not to pass out, but he lost consciousness, and his arm slid down to his side, leaving the cell phone on top of his face.

Officer Hall finished writing the information on the orange sticker, walked over to the Escort, and stuck it on the rear window. He glanced around the area.

Officer Dobbs completed the violation notice: 24 hours to move the car or a tow truck would move it at the driver's expense and heavy fines would ensue. He put the window down and handed it to his partner. "Here."

Officer Hall took the notice from his partner. "What? Are you stuck in there?"

Officer Dobbs grumbled, "You're out there already."

"You get the next one we find." Officer Hall attached the notice to the driver's window. As he returned to the squad car, he noticed a blanket at the side of the road. "People are so disgusting. What do they think this highway is?" He yelled to his partner, "Pop the trunk." When he bent down, that is when he heard the ringing and music. He left the blanket and headed toward the ditch.

"What are you doing now?" Officer Dobbs called out.

"I hear something."

Officer Dobbs left the squad car and ran to catch up to his partner. "Sounds like a cell phone."

Tony awoke and heard male voices. I'll be rescued, he thought. His phone was playing music, but he knew he had not pushed the button to make that happen. He saw the name, Robin, on the lit screen just before he fell asleep again.

Officer Hall pulled out his flashlight and scanned the area where he had heard the musical sounds. He spotted a large, black bag and walked cautiously to it. The music grew louder, and then it stopped. The officer knelt down over the bag, aimed his flashlight into the ripped area, and slowly looked inside the hole. He saw a cell phone on top of something that looked like flesh. Hall lifted the cell phone and gasped when he saw the bloody, swollen face. "Oh, ugh!" After vomiting along side the bag, he looked to Dobbs. "It's a dead body. Wait a minute." He shoved the cell phone into his pocket and knelt down. Hall yanked the toggle down, unzipped the bag, and placed his two fingers along the victim's neck. There was a dangerously weak pulse. "Dobbs, call for an ambulance!"

Tony felt the officer place a hand on his chest. He heard him say, "You're going to be all right." Thank you, God, he thought with the relief of knowing that he would not die like a piece of garbage tossed into a ditch. He tried to thank the officer. "Ah," was the only sound he was able to muster.

Hall became excited. "What is your name? Who did this to you?"

"Ah," Tony uttered again and then slipped into unconsciousness once more.

After the ambulance left with the body, Officer Hall and Dobbs bagged the blanket and the body bag and placed them in the trunk of their patrol car. They scanned the area for any further evidence. Officer Hall found the gasoline can, bagged it, and placed it into the trunk. Officer Dobbs called the tow company and the crime unit. Then they sat in their patrol car and waited.

Twenty minutes later, a detective from the crime unit arrived. He glanced around the area, drank a cup of coffee from his thermos, and questioned the officers. After jotting down some notes, he took the blue blanket, the black bag, and the empty gasoline can from the police officers' trunk. He placed all the items into his car and left.

Officer Hall and Officer Dobbs waited now for the tow truck. This is when Officer Hall remembered the victim's cell phone was still in his pocket. "I forgot to give him the phone."

"We'll leave it at the station. He can pick it up there."

Hall punched a few of the buttons. "The phone's dead. I should have tried it earlier."

"Give it to me. I'll take it home. I have a phone just like that," Dobbs said. "I'll plug it in and call one of the victim's family members. I'll find out who he is."

"That's the crime units' job."

"That detective didn't even put up any crime tape. Do you think he's going to make this phone a priority? He didn't even ask for it."

Officer Hall looked worried. "It's not just a phone; it's evidence, too."

"I know, but it's also a life line to a relative. If that were you in that ditch, would you really want your phone on a table in the crime unit for two or three days? Wouldn't you rather have your relatives notified right away?"

"Yeah, you're right. Here, take it. Call me when you know something." He reluctantly handed the cell phone over to his partner.

Dobbs put it into his pocket. "Our shift is over."

"What about the Escort?" Hall asked.

"We can't wait all night."

"We have to wait."

Dobbs called the tow company again. "Jim, what's going on? Where's our tow truck?" He paused for a second, listening. "So, send us a different truck."

When he ended the call, Hall asked, "What's the story?"

"Auto accidents, engine trouble, no trucks available, just name it. We're looking at a couple of hours."

"Shut your eyes. I'll keep watch."

"If we put a wheel lock on it, no one could take it, and we could go home."

"We don't have one."

"Our friend Larry does."

"What makes you think that a meter reader is going to come out here at this time?"

"He owes me a favor. Hell, I just loaned him twenty dollars at the bowling alley last night."

"We'll get into trouble."

"From who? The chief's not going to find out about it. Larry won't say anything to anyone."

"What about the tow company?"

"They don't care. Jim's got his hands full."

"All right."

Officer Dobbs called Larry, and as he had anticipated, his friend agreed to put a wheel lock on the Escort for him. Dobbs patted his partner on the shoulder. "Problem solved."

"I still don't know about this," Officer Hall, sighed.

"Look, which ever one shows up first, Larry or the tow truck driver, I'm leaving."

His friend arrived twenty minutes later and put the wheel lock on the Escort. After he left, Dobbs smiled. "Our shift is over."

Officer Hall shook his head. "You're going to get us in trouble, John."

"What do you want to do: wait here three more hours? We have the report to write yet, and Billy has a ball game tomorrow."

"Is he pitching?"

"Yeah, are you going to come?"

"Sure."

CHAPTER 18

Still Missing

It was a little after 2:00 a.m., Sunday, when Robin was crying in the women's bathroom at the diner. She cried harder as she analyzed her own thoughts. He's dead. Tony can't answer the phone. Why did I bother to call him? Tears slid down her face as she realized that her husband would never again talk to her. Slowly, she returned her cell phone to her purse.

Robin rejoined Tim and Craig at the table. They were the only customers in the restaurant. Tim removed more ice from Robin's glass and refilled his napkin to create another icepack for his swollen eye. The lid was purple and his eyebrow a greenish blue.

Craig drank another sip of his coffee. "Uncle Tony, I remember now. We…"

"Who's we?"

"Todd and me. We um…"

"Who's Todd?"

"My friend. We were leaving a graduation party at this chick's house, and we passed my ex-girlfriend on the side of the highway. Her car was broke down, and so we gave her and her friends a ride. I remember now where we were at."

"Let's go." Tim threw money down on the table and hustled Craig out of his seat. He guided him back to the truck. Before getting in on the passenger side, Tim turned to Robin and shoved his right index finger into her chest. "Make sure you stay right behind us."

Robin entered her car. She rubbed the tender area where he'd bruised her. She quickly started her car and followed them.

Craig drove the truck onto the highway. After a short distance, he exited, traveled a few side streets, and stopped in front of a house. "This was the last place we were."

"You said the bag was along the highway."

"It is, but this is where we were last; then we got on the highway."

"Get there then. I don't need a fricken tour of where you and your damn friend went."

Craig sped back to the highway. "I remember we drove this way."

"What kind of car did your ex-girlfriend have?"

"A blue Escort."

Craig drove for thirty minutes down the stretch of highway as Tim scanned the roadside for a broken down vehicle. "Craig, are you sure?"

"Oh, wait, man, I remember now. I think I drove through the turn around."

"What turn around?"

"The median," Craig answered sounding guilty.

Craig pulled off the highway and back on heading south. They traveled an hour. Just when Tim was ready to strangle Craig, the teen flung out his arm and pointed. "There's her car."

He pulled the SUV off the road and parked behind Becky's car. "This is it. The bag's off in the ditch over there."

The truck's headlights shone on the blue Escort. Tim dug out a flashlight from beneath the seat. "Get out, Craig," he ordered. "Follow me." The two walked quickly. "Robin, fix your headlights on the ditch," Tim yelled.

After a few seconds of scouting the area, Tim hollered. "I don't see anything."

Robin rushed down into the ditch and stood beside her nephew. She shook her head, "Me either."

Craig threw his hands up. "I don't know. This is weird. 'Cause, I promise you, it was right here where Todd and I rolled it off the truck. Honest, Uncle Tony."

Tim walked up and down the ditch. The grass and weeds were flat as though something heavy had crushed them. "I don't see it." He marched up to Craig. "Where's it at?" he yelled into the boy's face.

"I don't know," Craig cried. "It was here, honest." He moved over next to his aunt.

Tim walked back up onto the side of the highway. He examined the ground near his truck and the abandoned car. There were plenty of fresh shoeprints and two long lines in the dirt.

Robin wrapped one arm around Craig. "It's okay, dear. Don't worry."

"Get up here," Tim bellowed.

Robin and Craig walked quickly up to him. They now saw the shoeprints and lines.

"Whose car is that?" Tim snapped.

"Becky's. It broke down."

Tim looked at the car and noticed the orange sticker on the window. "Go home, Robin."

"I'll drive Craig home," she said. Her voice was shaky.

"No." He walked toward Craig. "Someone called my mother and pretended to be my...me. Was it you, Craig, playing more games with us?" He jabbed his left fist into Craig's side and at the same time dropped the flashlight. "You have my cell phone."

Robin spun her nephew's body away from Tim. "Stop it."

"I don't know what you're talking about," Craig insisted.

"Did you call my mother?"

"No."

"You know what was in that bag, don't you?"

"No, I don't. Honest, I don't."

Robin started walking him to her car. She continued to keep her arm wrapped around him.

"Let him go, Robin."

"He doesn't know anything. Leave him alone."

"Let him go."

"No. I'm driving him home." She let him go. "Hurry, get into the car!"

Craig ran for the car, but he was not fast enough. Tim gripped his shoulder in one hand and whirled his torso around. He twisted the front of the boy's shirt into a knot that he squeezed inside his fist. "What do you know?"

"Nothing," he cried.

"Where'd you go after you returned the truck? Where'd you go?"

"My friends picked me up in a van, and I passed out and slept. I just woke up before they dropped me off at home."

"Who else saw that bag?"

"Todd."

"Who's he?"

"I told you, he's my friend."

Tim made a fist and held it up to Craig's face. Waving it in front of him, he glared into his eyes.

Craig backed away from him. "Todd might have it. I didn't see your phone, but Todd probably did, and he probably took it, too. Yeah, it was Todd. He's the one that pushed that bag into the ditch. I can drive you over to see Todd." Craig was shaking.

"Follow us, Robin." Tim marched Craig to the truck.

"No, this is crazy. Whoever put the sticker on that car, has it. Look, there's a lock on that wheel." The flashlight that Tim had dropped was shinning on the wheel lock. "I'm taking him home. Go get in the car, Craig," she ordered.

Tim still had a tight hold on the boy's shirt. "No one is going anywhere."

"Uncle Tony, why don't we just go to the police station and ask if they have the bag?"

Robin shut her eyes in anticipation of Tim's reaction to the notion of police being involved. She wished she could have warned her nephew to be quiet.

Tim unknotted the teen's shirt and shoved him toward Robin's car. Craig tumbled backwards hitting his back hard against the hood. As the boy tried to recover from the sudden impact, Tim lunged after him with both fists in the air.

Robin saw Tim's fists heading forcefully into her nephew's face. She quickly picked the flashlight up off the ground and began pounding on Tim's back with it. "Leave him alone. Stop! Stop!"

Tim barely felt Robin hitting him, but he stopped when he saw the headlights of a tow truck pulling off the side of the road just in front of the Escort. Craig fell on the ground; blood poured from his nose and lips. One eye was already starting to swell. Tim bent down pretending to examine one of the tires. Then quickly, he climbed into the truck. "Get up. Get in the truck."

Robin ran to her nephew who was slowly pulling himself up from the ground. She wrapped her arms around him and helped him get inside the back of the SUV.

"Lay down," Tim whispered harshly.

Craig followed his instructions, and Robin ran back to her car, so that she would not lose Tim when he drove off. She was worried about what he would do to Craig. What kind of aunt would involve her nephew in a life or death situation? What kind of mother would put her unborn baby at risk? A weak one, she thought. A woman who does not know what to do about the nightmare that had suddenly engulfed her whole life, she answered, crying.

The driver of the tow truck walked to the back of the rig and eyed Tim. "Everything all right?"

"I thought I had a flat. It looks okay though. We're fine. Thanks." Tim nodded to him and smiled. "Bye."

CHAPTER 19

Billy's Game

On Sunday at 4:30 a.m., Officer John Dobbs entered his home. He quietly removed his shoes and set them by the door.

Billy woke up. He liked seeing his father in his uniform. "Dad, did you catch any bad guys today?"

Officer Dobbs locked the back door and turned to his eleven-year old son. "What are you doing up, slugger?"

"Mom said I had to talk to you to get my honor roll money."

Now, John noticed that Billy was holding his brown wallet with the cowboy printed on it. "All right, Son, how much do I owe you?"

"You and Mom said that you'd give me $10.00 for each A. I have five of them," he stated proudly pulling out his report card from his wallet. He unfolded it. "See, five A's."

"Can't this wait until later? You need your sleep. How are you going to hit home runs if you fall asleep at the game?

Go on back to bed. I'll see you at lunch time." He patted Billy on the shoulder.

He watched his son walk toward his bedroom with his head down and shoulders sagging. "Hey, wait a minute, slugger. I'm playing with you. I've got your money right here." He opened his wallet and gave Billy a fifty-dollar bill. "There you go, slugger. Your mom and I are proud of you. Now, go back to sleep and grow."

Billy smiled. He picked up an ink pen off the table and wrote Honor roll on his bill.

"Son, don't write on money. Put it away."

He happily stuck the fifty into his wallet. "Here, Dad, keep my report card. You and Mom can frame it and put it on the wall."

"Don't you think you'll earn more of these?"

"Nope, that was hard to do. Goodnight." He ran off to bed.

John laughed at him and set the report card on the coffee table for his wife to see when she woke up. Then, John crept into his own bedroom, unplugged his wife's cell phone, and carried the cord into the living room. He pulled the victim's cell phone from his pocket and plugged it into the charger. Nothing happened. The battery was completely dead. Leaving it there, he began his early morning routine: hang his hat, belt, and holster on the hook on the kitchen wall; carefully unload his 9mm Glock and lock it in its case; place it on the top shelf of the cupboard over the refrigerator; quietly, walk into the bathroom; brush his teeth; remove his uniform; wash up; creep into his bedroom and slip into bed beside his wife.

Billy knew his routine, also. He lay in his bed listening and waiting. When he thought his father was asleep, he snuck into the kitchen, placed a chair up next to the refrigerator, climbed up, and opened the cupboard above it. He removed the key from the coffee cup that was next to the gun case.

Then he unlocked it and carefully removed his father's gun. After climbing down from the chair, he removed his father's hat, belt, and holster from the hook. He placed the hat on his head and hooked the belt and holster around his waist.

Quietly, he carried the gun into the bathroom. Billy placed the 9mm Glock into the holster. Staring into the mirror, he straightened his father's hat with his left hand and placed his right hand on the handle of the weapon. Billy quickly yanked the pistol out of the holster and pointed it at the large mirror. "Stop or I'll shoot," he whispered. The hat slid to the side of his head. The gun felt heavy. Carefully, he set it on the counter and unhooked the handcuffs from the belt. He latched one cuff onto his left wrist and whispered, "You're under arrest." Then he unlocked it with the key. The boy placed the gun in the holster and pretended he had the quickest draw in the world. "Stop or I'll shoot," he whispered and drew the gun quickly, once again aiming it at the mirror. After ten minutes, he grew tired of his game and put his playthings away. He returned everything back to its usual place.

On the way to his bedroom, he heard a low beep sound and discovered the cell phone setting on the end table in the living room. Billy walked over to it and picked it up. There was a message on it: charged. Having wanted one of these for a long while, he pushed several buttons, looked at numbers and names, read the selection of ring tones, and glanced at the saved pictures of strangers. Soon, he learned how to work the camera and took pictures of the living room.

"What are you doing?" His eight year-old brother, Jeff, walked up behind him.

Billy jumped. "Don't sneak up on me like that."

"What do you have?"

"A cell phone."

"Wow. Where'd you get it?"

"Dad brought it home."

"I'm telling."

"I'm going to put it back. I'm just borrowing it."

"Oh."

"Let's call someone. Want to?"

"Sure." Jeff jumped up on the couch.

Billy pushed the button menu and then the contacts. There appeared a list of names and numbers.

"I want to go first," Jeff yelled.

"Shh, quiet. I'm going first."

"You always go first for everything."

"Shh, quiet. You're going to wake everyone up. I'm going first 'cause I'm the oldest."

"No, you're not. Taylor is."

"She's not up, so that makes me the oldest right now."

"Oh." He thought for a few seconds. "Why can't the youngest go first?"

"Shh! Keep your voice down. I think Mom's up."

Billy and Jeff quickly ran back into their bedroom, jumped into their beds, and pretended to be sleeping.

The door opened. "Boys, are you up?" their mother called out in a whisper.

They stayed quiet. She closed the door and walked back into her bedroom.

Billy sat up. "That was close."

"Let's go." Jeff was already out of bed and at the doorway.

"You have to wait. You have to give Mom time to fall asleep again."

Jeff climbed back into his bed on the bottom bunk. He waited.

Five minutes later, Billy leaned over the guardrail and whispered, "Okay, let's go," but there was no response. He leaned over more and saw his brother sleeping.

CHAPTER 20

Stranger

It was Sunday morning and Jill planned to sleep in, but a constant knocking woke her from a deep sleep. She didn't even recall what she had been dreaming about, nor did she care. All she knew now was that someone had invaded her sleep. What is that noise? She demanded to know and vowed to make the lunatic pay for stealing her shuteye. Listening hard, Jill realized the noise was coming from next door. She sat up in bed and made an angry face. "What the hell is the matter with those people?" she muttered to herself.

Jill donned a pink robe and orange slippers. Then, she opened the apartment door and peered out. She saw an elderly woman persistently knocking on the neighbor's door. "If they don't answer, it's because they're not home," she yelled at her.

The woman abruptly stopped knocking and practically ran to Jill. "Do you know where they are?" she asked frantically.

"No."

"Oh, I have to get a hold of them. Something is wrong."

"What?"

"Could I use your phone?"

"Well, I…um…I guess so. Sure, come in." Jill pointed to the phone in the kitchen. "It's right there." She watched the woman rush to it and push buttons. Maybe the neighbors beat each other to death; no, I would have heard that, she thought. Looking at the clock on the stove, she decided it had better be something damn good to awaken her at 4:30 in the morning. Jill eavesdropped on the frantic stranger. It did not seem that anyone was answering her call.

The woman set the phone down. With exasperation in her voice, she said, "I don't know what to do." Without an invitation, the gray haired woman sat down in a chair at the kitchen table.

Jill realized now that she, herself, had a problem. What was the proper procedure for getting a stranger out of your kitchen? She was not sure, but she knew that letting the stranger in was her first error.

"Tony called me." Her voice was shaky.

"Did he threaten you?"

"What?" The woman looked bewildered by the question. "He's my son."

"Oh, you're his mother?" Jill said with relief.

"Yes, and last night he called me. I think he was hurt. I think he said that he was injured. He sounded bad. I've been calling and calling, but no one answers."

"The last time I saw your son was last night. He was fighting with a man in the parking lot."

"Oh, no," she cried.

"He wasn't hurt; the other guy was. Your son left with some guy in a truck. Robin was there, but she left in her own car."

"What kind of truck was it?"

"An SUV."

"Tim has a truck. He hasn't been home lately. He doesn't have a phone, so I can't call him."

"Who's Tim?"

"Tony's twin brother."

"He has a twin?"

"Yes, I guess he doesn't talk about him. They don't get along."

Jill turned the coffee maker on and sat in a chair across from the woman. "Would you like a cup of coffee?"

"Oh, thank you. That would be nice. I haven't slept since I received that phone call last night." She sneezed.

"Bless you. What time was that?"

"It was just after midnight. I answered the phone, but I couldn't hear who it was, so I looked at my caller ID, and it was Tony's name and cell phone number. It sounded like his voice. I couldn't make out what he was saying. I guess we had a bad connection. I hung up and called him back, but he didn't answer. I know they're on vacation, but they didn't say they were going any place. I phoned Robin's cell phone, but she didn't answer either. I even left a message. I phoned the police."

"What did they say?"

"They said they couldn't help me. I don't know what to do."

"Well, Tony was walking when he left the parking lot and that was past midnight."

"Are you sure that was him?" She sneezed.

"Bless you. Yes. Robin was with him. Like I said, they left in separate vehicles, but they were both down there during the fight."

"Well, maybe I'm worried over nothing."

Jill poured them each a cup of coffee. She set out the creamer and sugar. "What about your other son, Tim? You said that you haven't been able to get a hold of him. You must be a wreck."

"I am. Tim never said that he was going anywhere. I know he talked with Robin on the phone, but he couldn't have visited her. Tony would never allow that."

"Why not?"

Tim's been in prison for the last seven years." She lowered her head shamefully. "He made a few mistakes." The woman's face wore sudden lines of stress that appeared across her forehead. "He stole a car and took it across the state line." She took a gulp of her coffee. "Well, he did have a gun, but he let the driver go. He didn't hurt anyone." She took another gulp of coffee and added the word, "much." The distressed mother shook her head. "He pistol whipped the man." She drained her coffee cup. "I couldn't look at that man and his family in court. My son deserved prison. Sometimes he scares me."

Jill thought the same way about Tony: he scared her. It was hard for her to imagine that he could have a twin more awful than he was.

"Now, Tony, he's nothing like Tim. He's sweet. I don't know how they could have turned out so different."

Jill decided not to disillusion the woman and tell her that Tony beats his wife and cheats on her. She refilled their coffee cups. "Why don't you give me your phone number, and I'll call you when I see Tony or Robin. This way, you won't worry about them."

She smiled. "That is nice of you. It's good that Tony has such a nice neighbor. Have you lived here long?" She sneezed.

"Bless you. No, I don't live here. I'm apartment sitting for Laura, a friend of mine. I've actually only been in here for a couple of days, but I have met Tony and Robin. Your son introduced himself to me out in the parking lot a couple of mornings ago. He seemed friendly."

"Oh, he is. He's always been that way." She sneezed.

"Bless you."

"I don't know why I'm sneezing so much."

"Maybe it's the dust. I haven't really cleaned much." Jill handed her a box of tissue.

The lady took one. "You don't have a cat, do you?"

"My friend does. Is that what you're allergic to?"

"Yes. I am."

"Well, that explains all the sneezing."

She sneezed. "My son, Tony, is allergic to cats, too, but not his brother."

"Bless you. So twins aren't allergic to the same things?"

"No. One pediatrician told me that it had something to do with the developmental stages of the embryos. Another one said that the boys had encountered different things in their childhoods that caused them to build up different immunities. I don't know which one to believe. Anyway, I should go. You have been kind enough to let me use your phone, and here I am rattling on about allergies."

Jill handed her a tissue. "I remember, Robin told me that she wanted a cat, but couldn't have one because of Tony's allergies."

"I didn't know she wanted a cat. I've been waiting for her to want a baby."

"Oh." Jill looked on the counter for a writing utensil. That is when she noticed the key chain with the picture of the redheaded woman on it. She threw it in the junk drawer, pulled out a piece of paper and a pen, and handed them to Tony's mother.

Ms. Henkerson wrote down her name and phone number. She sneezed again and then handed the paper and pen to Jill. "Thank you for the coffee, oh, and letting me use your phone."

"Bless you. You're welcome." Jill looked at the paper and read, Lilly Henkerson. She glanced at the phone number. "I'll call you when I see them, Lilly."

CHAPTER 21

Suspicious Behavior

At 9:00 a.m., on Sunday, Jill woke up in the recliner where she had fallen asleep. Kittykay was snuggled in her lap, sleeping. "I'm not much of a pet lover, but you are beginning to grow on me." Now, that she was awake for good, it came to her attention that Kittykay's litter box needed cleaning.

After showering and dressing, Jill lifted the garbage bag from the container under the sink and carried it into Kittykay's room. I can do this, she thought. Jill spotted a lump amongst the sandy particles in the litter box. She knelt down, picked up the scooper, and fished it out and plopped it into the trash bag. "Okay, that wasn't so bad."

On her way to the dumpster, she noticed an old, green, rusty SUV parked in the same space as last night. The Henkersons had returned home.

Jill tossed the trash bag into the dumpster and ran back into the building. As she hurried down the hallway, Robin walked quickly past her. Jill turned and ran after her.

"Is everything all right?" Jill yelled out, trying to catch Robin's attention.

"Yes," Robin answered back and continued walking out the doors. She quickened her pace.

Jill walked faster and followed her out of the building. "I'm only asking because your mother-in-law came by this morning. She said that she couldn't get a hold of you or your husband. I was just about to call her and let her know that you're home."

Robin stopped walking. She turned and faced Jill. "What is it that you were saying about my mother-in-law?"

"Your mother-in-law was worried about you and your husband. She was at your door this morning, but you obviously weren't home. She used my phone and had a cup of coffee with me. She was very worried about you and your husband. She said Tony called her from his cell phone last night, but she said that she couldn't understand him. I guess probably a bad connection. Anyway, she wants one of you to call to say everybody is fine."

"Really?"

"Yes."

"It's only nine o' clock now. What time did she come by?"

"Around four-thirty."

"Really?"

"Yes." Jill waited for Robin's explanation as to where they were and what the strange phone call from Tony meant. She hoped, also, that she would explain the fight in the parking lot last night.

"I'll call her. Thanks." Robin began walking.

Jill followed her through the parking lot. "I don't want to pry or anything, but what's going on? What was that fight last night?"

Robin continued to walk to her car. "What?"

"You know, the fight in the parking lot between your husband and the guy who looked like the Hulk."

Robin opened her car door and gave Jill a bewildered look. "You saw that?"

"Hard not to; I mean, it was right there for all the neighbors to see. I'm sure half of the neighbors called the police." Jill placed her hand on the car door. "I told your mother-in-law that your husband looked okay after the fight. I mean, he was walking, so I assumed he was okay. Is he?" Secretly, she hoped he wasn't.

"Yes, he's okay," Robin answered, sounding annoyed. She sat in the driver's seat, looked at Jill's hand, and then to her eyes. "I'm sorry, but I have to go somewhere."

"Oh, right." As Jill was about to remove her hand, she noticed that Robin had bruises up by her wrists near the sleeves of her sweater. Now, she knew why this woman was wearing a sweater in the hot weather. "Like I said, I don't want to pry, but is everything all right?"

Robin burst into tears. "No."

Finally, Jill thought. Robin is going to admit the abuse she has been enduring and get some help.

"It's my nephew. He's been hurt, and I have to take him home. I'll call my mother-in-law, thank you." She pulled lightly on the door, but Jill did not move her hand.

The apartment door opened slowly, and both women watched Craig walk out. His right eye was swollen almost shut, and his lip was bruised and puffy.

Jill gasped. "What happened?" She removed her hand from the car door and walked to Craig. Robin took the quick opportunity to shut her driver's side door and lock it.

Craig ignored her and walked to the front passenger side of his aunt's car. He pulled up his sagging pants and opened the door.

Jill turned and walked quickly back to Robin's side of the car and knocked on the window. "What happened to your nephew?"

As soon as Craig climbed into the front passenger seat and closed the door, Robin started her car and put the window down a slight crack. "He was in an auto accident. We have to go," she said, and speedily backed out of the parking lot.

Jill watched the car drive off. "Okay, that was odd," she muttered to herself. As she walked back to her apartment, she thought about what she could do to help. Jill cell phoned Lilly Henkerson and explained that she had seen her daughter-in-law. She decided not to worry the woman further by telling her about Robin's nephew. Lilly's main concern was her son. Had she seen him? She confessed that she had not. With phone in hand, Jill walked over to Tony's apartment and knocked on the door.

Tim opened it. He had a cigarette hanging out of his mouth, and he looked surprised to see Jill.

"Sorry to bother you, but your mother has been worried about you. She wants to make sure you're all right. She's on the phone. Here you go." Jill held her cell phone out to him.

He looked shocked as though she had held out a poisonous snake. "My Mom? What?"

Jill pulled the phone back. "I know this is weird, but she was over this morning, and you weren't home. She came over to use my phone, and I told her I would call her when I saw you. I see you, so here." Again, she held the phone out to him.

Slowly, he took it from her and held it up to the side of his head. "Mom?"

Moments later, after Lilly had stopped talking, Tim replied, "I don't know, but I'm fine. I don't want to use the neighbor's cell minutes up."

"That's okay. It's free on the weekends. Go ahead, talk," Jill said loudly so that Lilly would hear.

Many minutes later, Tim spoke again. "I don't know why. It was a prankster, Mom. Quit worrying about it. I'm busy. I'll call you back." He pushed the end button.

"Um, your mom said that your brother has a truck. Do you have a truck or is that your brother's SUV that I saw you in earlier?"

He was stumped. "It's a friend's. I'm just borrowing it to move some stuff."

Jill had not shut the apartment door all the way, and Kittykay slinked out. Jill saw her. "Hey, you get back in there."

The cat looked at her and then picked up speed and ran between Tim's legs and into the apartment. Jill headed toward Tim as he backed up to go after the cat.

Tim turned quickly to bar Jill from heading any farther into the apartment, but she had already made it into the living room. "Stop. I'll get your cat. Stay here," he ordered.

Frightened by his harshness, Jill backed up into the hallway. "You know, I will just wait out here."

He moved quickly near her. "Here, take your phone." After handing her the phone, he squished his cigarette out in a coffee cup that was on the kitchen counter, and then he headed toward the bedroom in pursuit of the cat.

Tim saw the cat crawl under Robin's bed. He reached down under the foot of the bed, grabbed the cat by its tail, and yanked it out.

The cat meowed sharply causing Jill to rush into the bedroom. "What happened?"

"Nothing," Tim shouted. He let the tail go, grasped the cat under its belly, and lifted it in the air.

Jill hurried after him. "Let me have her." This is when Jill noticed a squished orange in the floor and the busted bedroom doorframe.

"I've got her." He turned around holding the cat and walked past Jill and to the door. "Here," he said holding the cat out in the hallway.

Jill hurried out into the hallway and quickly took Kittykay from him. She gently held her and petted her. "It's okay. You'll be all right," she said speaking softly. Prior to him having grabbed the cat, she was planning to scold her, but not now.

"What happened to your nephew?" she asked, accusingly.

Tony was quick with his response. "He fell."

"Off of what?"

He paused for a few moments as though he were trying to think of an answer. "A car. He was goofing around with his friends."

"That's odd. Your wife said that he was in an auto accident."

"Same thing. It involved a vehicle. You have your cat now."

"Did you take him to the hospital?"

"His mother's a nurse. Robin's taking him home to her. Why are you asking me all these questions?" he asked angrily.

"I was just concerned about his welfare."

"Don't be," he said in a threatening voice.

She was suddenly frightened that he would hit her. Quickly, she headed to Laura's apartment with Kittykay.

He slammed his apartment door. "Nosey broad," he griped under his breath but loud enough for her to hear.

Jill entered Laura's apartment, closed the door, and remained standing in front of it for a few seconds feeling used and upset. She realized that the strange phone call that Lilly Henkerson had received bothered her more than it did Robin or Tony. She set Kittykay down and phoned Laura. The only thing that Jill thought could possibly make her feel better was to tell someone else about her feelings, and since these were Laura's neighbors, she seemed the likely candidate.

CHAPTER 22

P's And Q's

An hour later, Laura met Jill at the International House of Pancakes. After placing food orders, Laura asked, "Okay, so you're upset because no one else is?"

Jill leaned back in the booth. "I guess."

"Why do you care? It's not even any of your business."

"Don't you think it's strange though? What if someone called your mother, and it sounded like you? Plus, you sounded like you were hurt."

"My mother? Are you kidding? She freaks out if I'm late."

"Okay, so you see what I mean. This would upset you."

"Me, yes, but not all people react the same."

"Tony didn't even care that someone upset his mother."

"Maybe his mother's crazy. She hallucinates: hears phone calls that never take place."

"No, she seemed normal enough. She sneezed a lot, but that was because she's allergic to cats. Actually, the cat was in its room."

"That won't matter. Cat hair and cat dander can cause it."

"You know, another odd thing is that when Tony held the cat, he didn't sneeze. His mother and his wife said that he was allergic to cats, so why didn't he sneeze?"

"Some people just get puffy eyes, and they can't breathe."

"Something's not right. I don't know what it is, but something is definitely not right. The nephew was beat up looking."

"You said he was in an auto accident."

"Yeah, but why not wash the blood off, bandage the injuries, you know, get cleaned up?"

"Didn't you say that kid was drunk the last time you saw him?"

"Yeah."

"He was in a drunken stupor, that's why."

"Why didn't Robin clean him up?"

"Jill, come out of their world and get back into your own. Whatever is going on over there, it doesn't involve you; so don't get involved."

"Am I supposed to let Robin continue to get pounded on? What if he kills her? What will I do? Wait, and be one of those neighbors who says, they were such a quiet couple. I never would have guessed he'd kill her. Now, that would be a big lie. I would have to say, they fought like wild animals, and I thought any minute he would do her in."

"You can't make her want help."

"But, I know what's going on. I feel like I should do something."

"You should mind your P's and Q's. My father always said that."

"What does that mean?"

"Mind your own business."

"What does P's and Q's have to do with that message?"

"That, I don't know."

Jill added more sugar to her coffee and stirred it. "There was a key chain with a picture of a woman in it. Did you leave that on the counter the other day when you stopped in?"

"I found it on the stairs when I was taking out the cat litter. I left a message on the eraser board in the mailroom."

"A keychain without a key?"

"Maybe the picture is valuable."

"I tossed it in your junk drawer. Now, I know how that junk got in there. You need to quit picking up junk that you find lying around."

"Mind your P's and Q's."

"Stop saying that. It sounds weird."

"You need it. You have a problem with getting involved in other people's business."

Jill put her head down. "Wow. Why do I do that?"

"Your fiancé has been busy lately, and you're just bored. Boredom makes people do crazy things."

"Maybe you're right. Robin married that guy, and if she lets him pound on her, what business is it of mine? Why should I care if her drunken nephew is injured? It's not my business if someone's mother is getting prank calls. Why should I care? You're right; none of it is my business, so how did I get involved?"

"You overstepped your boundaries."

"How did I do it?"

"I don't know, but you did. You'll just have to try and be more aware of it when it happens the next time, and then stop yourself."

"Right. I will. I'll mind my own P's and Q's, whatever the hell those things are."

Their food arrived, and they began to eat. Jill's cell phone sounded with music. Quickly, she dug it out of her purse. She looked at the number on its screen. "I don't recognize this number. I better get this and find out who it is. Sorry."

Laura nodded an okay and continued chewing her bacon. She ate, and at the same time, she read Jill's facial expressions: surprise, now shock, dismay, worry. The call ended with Jill looking terribly guilty.

"Who was it?"

"It was Tony's mother."

"You gave her your cell number?"

"No. She got it when I phoned her this morning. She has caller ID."

"What did she want?"

"Nothing."

"Cut it out. I know it was something. I can tell. Now, what was it?"

"Well, she wants me to spy on her son. She thinks that, well, this is going to sound crazy, but she thinks that he's missing."

"You said that he talked to her on your phone this morning."

"He did."

"She's a nut case."

"She thinks that maybe that was her other son, Tim: Tony's twin."

"What?"

"I told you that she said he had a twin."

Laura shook her head. "No, you didn't."

"Oh. I thought I did."

"It doesn't matter. Jill, you call her back and tell her that you won't do it; that it's none of your business what her sons are doing."

"She thinks Tony is hurt, and she was crying on the phone. How am I supposed to call her back and tell her I won't help her?"

"They're her sons. Let her find out who's who."

"She's afraid to."

"Why?" Laura sipped her coffee.

"She's afraid of Tim. He's an ex-con, and sometimes he's violent. I guess he nearly killed a guy once."

Laura's coffee spilled down her chin as she quickly yanked her cup back. "What? Are you crazy? You'll get killed. Are you kidding me? This is crazy!"

"Well, what should I do?"

"Not a damn thing. I just told you."

"You mean just ignore it all?"

"Right. It doesn't involve you."

"But, I know the Henkersons."

"No, you don't. They're my neighbors, not yours, and I barely know them."

"You said that they were a nice couple. You're the one who sent me over to their apartment with that marriage counseling card."

"Exactly, because, like you, I thought I knew them a little bit, and now, I realize I didn't know anything about them. I got involved when I shouldn't have."

"No, you got me involved."

Laura let out a heavy sigh. "Let's just forget the whole thing. Look at your pancakes; they're cold. You're not eating. Don't ever call that woman back. Stay away from the Henkersons' apartment. Let's just eat our breakfast."

Jill nodded her head. "Okay. I'm going to mind my own business as of right now."

CHAPTER 23

The Greenways

"Fred! Fred!" Edna cried.

On Sunday morning, Fred had fallen asleep on the couch. All night long, he had been a caretaker: giving his wife her medicine, helping her to the bathroom, getting her water, sponging the sweat from her forehead, calling the hospital, and massaging her back. Now, after fifteen minutes of deep sleep, he awoke, startled.

Quickly, he felt for his eyeglasses on the arm of the couch. He put them on and saw the clock. It was 10:00 a.m. "I'm coming, Edna," he called out as he headed into the bedroom.

She was sitting up in her bed. "It hurts, Fred. It hurts to breathe," she cried.

"I'm right here." He took hold of his wife's hands.

Edna gasped for air, laboring for each breath that she took. Tears and fear were in her eyes. She pulled her frail hands away from him and touched her chest. "It hurts."

Fred hated to watch her suffer. Why? He asked God a thousand times in his mind. Why must she suffer like this?

"I'll phone the doctor again."

Edna cried and struggled to breathe. She looked to her husband for help.

He quickly punched in the number and waited. Prompt after prompt, he pushed buttons until he became exasperated. After speaking to a receptionist and a nurse, Fred finally had the doctor on the phone.

"I did give her the medicine. It's not working. She's in pain. You have to do something. How is she supposed to get rest if she can't sleep because of the pain?"

He shifted the phone to his other ear, so that he could massage his wife's back. "Can't you just give her something that works? I can't bring her up there. It's too much for her, and besides, we can't afford it. Can't you just call in another prescription to the pharmacy?"

After listening to the doctor's answer, Fred shook his head. "Fine, we'll come up there." He ended the call and quickly packed a small suitcase with one of Edna's nightgowns because she refused to wear the hospital's smocks. He tossed in her toothbrush, dentures, hairbrush, and sanitizing wash wipes. "Put your glasses on, sweetheart; we're going to the hospital."

Edna just kept trying to breathe. Her husband put her glasses on her and then her shoes. He wrapped a housecoat around her and helped her into the wheelchair. With a suitcase in one hand and the handle of the wheelchair in the other, he tried to make it to the doorway. The wheels would not move.

Fred set the suitcase down and shoved both hands on the brake lever. It was stuck. He bent down and looked his wife in the eyes. Sadly, he registered the pain he saw in them.

"Honey, I'm going to go and get Tony to help us. I'll be right back."

Fred walked up the stairs and to Tony's apartment. He knocked on the door and waited.

The door opened. "What'd ya want?" Tim asked sounding annoyed.

"Tony," Fred smiled. "My wife's wheelchair is stuck again. It's the brake again."

"Yeah, so?"

"I was hoping you would fix it again, like you did last month. I have to take Edna in to see the doctor. Her medicine isn't working."

"Sure. Just give me a sec." Tim closed the door. "I don't believe this shit," he muttered. He squished out his cigarette on the counter and left the apartment.

Tim followed Fred into his apartment. Edna was moaning loudly. Tim winced at the noises that she was making. Without a problem, he shoved the brake release lever.

"Thank you, Tony. I don't know how we'd manage without you." Fred pulled their extra apartment key off his key chain and handed it to Tim. "Here, Tony, just in case we don't return right away. Oh, and I didn't give Charlie any water yet."

Tim shoved the key into his pocket and glanced around the living room for a pet. "I'll do it for you."

Fred struggled, carrying the suitcase and pushing the wheelchair out through the doorway. The door banged into his arm, and the suitcase fell from his hand.

"Here, let me help you." Tim grabbed the suitcase and laid it on Edna's lap.

Edna cried out. "It hurts."

Fred removed the suitcase, wondering what had gotten into Tony. Why had he done that? After waiting a few seconds for Tony to offer to push the wheelchair or carry the suitcase even, Fred juggled his way down the hallway. "Would you mind locking up for us, Tony?"

"Not a problem."

He waited until the building doors closed, and then he stepped back inside their apartment and shut the door. Tim ransacked the place. They must have some money somewhere, he thought as he searched the bookshelves, checked the dresser drawers, and hunted through shoeboxes in their bedroom closet. He kicked the bed with his cowboy boot, sliding the mattress off the box spring just enough to see a black sock. Quickly, Tim grabbed it, looked inside, and found five hundred dollars. He stuffed the bills into his pocket and let the sock drop onto the floor. Then he pushed the mattress back in place and laughed. On his way out of the bedroom, he bumped the flourishing, green ivy and knocked it off the little table. The blue, ceramic pot, with the name Charlie painted on it, broke into pieces. The plant spilled out onto the bedroom carpet, and dirt fell into clumps around it. Tim walked through the dirt stepping on the plant. He scanned the living room and kitchen to see if there was anything worth taking. The television was the only thing that he thought he might be able to pawn, so he unplugged the cords and hoisted the set up on one shoulder. As Tim left, he made sure he locked the Greenway's apartment door.

CHAPTER 24

Accident Story

At 10:00 a.m. on Sunday, Robin sat across from her sister at the kitchen table. "I'm so sorry for not calling you earlier."

"I had to work an extra shift or I would have been here. Sometimes I feel like a terrible parent," Sharon replied.

"Accidents happen."

"Yes, but to steal a vehicle?"

"Well, I did say he could borrow my car. And, I forgot."

"But to take a truck that he found keys for. I swear he needs reform school."

"I better get going."

"Are you sure there wasn't any damage to your friend's truck?"

"It's nothing to worry about."

"What about the pole?"

"Nope. Everything is fine."

"I should probably get him a fresh ice pack. Help yourself to another cup of coffee. I'll be right back."

Robin felt terribly guilty about what happened to her nephew, but she knew that if she told Sharon the truth, she and her son would be in danger. It had taken hours to convince Tim not to kill Craig and to allow her to take him home. Craig promised not to say that his uncle hit him if in return, they would not say that he had been drinking.

Sharon returned to the kitchen. "He'll be all right. It looks like he'll be bruised for a couple of days though. I can't believe he wasn't wearing a seat belt. He knows I work in emergency. I've told him about people I've seen coming in there. Some are dead on arrival, but they would have lived had they been wearing a seatbelt. I just don't know how to get through to him, and then to find out that he took your friend's truck without permission."

Feeling very guilty, Robin replied, "I'm sure he's learned his lesson."

"He better have, or I'm shipping his defiant, lazy butt off to his father's. He keeps telling me that he is trying to get a job. I always come home, and he is lying down watching television or playing video games. He's wearing his shadow into the couch." She grabbed a bottle of water from the inside of the refrigerator. "I'm going to take this to him. I'll be right back."

When her sister disappeared from the kitchen, Robin let out a heavy breath full of tension. She lightly massaged her belly, thinking, I need to make a doctor appointment. If only Tim would leave, I could focus on you. As she softly patted her baby bump, her cell phone started playing a tune. Startled, she jumped and thought, I need to relax, or Sharon is going to get suspicious. It's probably my mother-in-law, Robin presumed while digging into her purse. Pulling out her phone, she glanced at the caller ID and inhaled sharply. "Tony!" she whispered and quickly pushed the talk button. Anticipating her husband's voice, Robin pressed the phone to her ear.

"I'm from the power company. Is your refrigerator running?" The boy laughed.

"What?"

"Is your refrigerator running?"

"Who is this? How did you get this phone? This is my husband's."

Sharon hurried into the kitchen. "What do you want?"

"Nothing."

"I thought you called me."

Robin stood up. "No, no, I didn't. I had a phone call." She listened into her phone, but the caller was gone.

"You look pale. Are you all right?"

"Yes, I'm fine."

Sharon turned her back to her sister while she poured herself another cup of coffee. "I'm glad that you didn't go to visit Mom. Now, you can spend some of your time off with me." She poured creamer into her cup. "Maybe, tomorrow, we can go shopping." When there was no response, she turned and eyed her sister. "Robin, you don't look good. Sit down."

Robin shoved her cell phone into her purse. "I'm fine." A dizzy feeling overtook her; a sudden hotness and then coldness swept through her. Both knees felt weak, and slowly she crumpled to the floor.

"Robin!" Sharon rushed to her.

She tried to pull herself up, but once again, the dizziness caused her to collapse. Helplessly, Robin remained sitting on the floor.

Sharon helped her back into the chair. "You passed out. What's the matter with you?"

Robin wanted to tell her sister everything and to cry on her shoulder, but she knew that Tim was right, she would be the one to go to prison for Tony's death. "Well, it's... I'm..."

Sharon saw bruises on Robin's wrists and pulled up her sleeves to reveal even more brown and blue spots. "Your arms are a mess! What happened?"

"I fell at work."

"How? Take off the sweater I want to see how bad it is."

"No."

"Robin, you know what I do for a living. Now, take off your sweater."

She removed her sweater. "It's nothing. It doesn't even hurt."

"Oh, your back's a mess. What happened?" Sharon pressed her hand against one of her sister's shoulder blades. "That doesn't hurt?"

Robin thought she would pass out from the pain. "No, I'm fine," she managed to say.

"How did you do this?"

She moved away from her sister's hands. "I slipped on some water on the floor at work."

"If I didn't know Tony was such a wonderful husband, I'd think he was beating you. Your bruises are so deep."

"I'm fine. It looks worse than it is."

"You passed out. You could be bleeding internally. Did you go to the hospital?"

"No, I'm fine."

"How could this have happened at work? You're on vacation."

"It happened on my last day there." She put her sweater back on.

"Passing out is a sign that something's wrong."

"I didn't pass out because of this. I'm pregnant."

"Pregnant! Oh. Honey, that's wonder…, but you fell. I want you to go to the hospital. I'll drive you."

"No. If anything is wrong, I can drive myself or have Tony take me."

"I can't believe he hasn't taken you already."

"I bruise easy, that's all."

"Well, you should still go see your doctor. Who are you using?" Sharon put her hand on her sister's belly. "Oh, I felt the baby kick."

"Dr. Chapes."

"Who's that? I never heard that name."

"New doctor."

"Why use someone new? I know some very good obstetricians. Did you get an ultrasound? They have them in 3D now. Is it a girl or boy?"

"No, I didn't get one yet. I don't know what it is. Would you do me a favor, Sis?"

"Sure."

"Keep it a secret. I haven't told anyone yet."

"Why not?"

"I want to surprise Tony."

"He doesn't know?"

"No. Our anniversary is coming up, and I thought the news would make it special."

"That's right. I forgot. This is what, your seventh year together?"

"Yes."

Okay, I won't say anything, but it will be difficult. You know I have a big mouth."

Robin's cell phone vibrated in her purse and played music. She became nervous.

"You can answer it. I don't mind."

"No, that's okay. Whoever it is will leave a message if it's important." She got up again, this time, more slowly. "I need to get going."

Sharon put her arm out to help Robin. "You need to eat right. You look anemic. Find something else to cover your arms. This sweater is too thick for summer. Are you getting enough sleep?"

"Not lately. Now, that I'm on vacation, I'll get my rest. Don't worry about me."

Sharon poured her sister a glass of orange juice and gave her a couple cubes of cheddar cheese. "Here, eat these. You need something."

"Thank you." Robin drank the juice and ate the cheese. Right away, she felt better.

"When can I tell everyone the news?" her sister asked excited.

"What news?"

"Wow, you really are out of it."

"Oh, the baby! You can tell everyone after I tell Tony."

"Well, hurry up and tell him and call me as soon as you do. Promise?"

"I promise."

Sharon walked Robin to her car. "Are you sure you're all right to drive?"

"I'm fine."

Once, she had driven out of her sister's sight, Robin stopped the car along the roadside and checked to see if the caller left a message. It was the same boy's voice once again inquiring about the refrigerator. She hit the call back button.

"Hello," the boy said.

She could hear giggling in the background. "Who are you?" she asked.

The boy ended the call. She called him again, but he wouldn't answer. Robin cried as she listened to her husband's voice: "This is Tony Henkerson. I'm away from my phone. Please, leave a message, and I'll return your call." Beep!

CHAPTER 25

The Deal

The buzzer sounded. Tim pushed the button next to the speaker on the wall in the kitchen. "Who is it?"

"Me. Are you going to let me in?"

It sounded like his brother's girlfriend. "Sandy?"

"Who else would it be?" she asked playfully.

He wondered what was going on as he buzzed her into the building and opened the apartment door for her. When she threw herself into his arms, he was happily surprised.

"I was hurt last night when you said that you never wanted to see me again."

Tim hugged her and accepted her kisses. "Let's go into the bedroom," he whispered.

Sandy giggled and let him lead the way. Then she stopped in front of the bed. Gazing into his eyes, she said, "Bo promised never to bother me or you again. Did Robin agree to the divorce?"

"Sweetie, let's talk about that later." He picked her up and heaved her into the air.

Sandy landed hard on the bed. "Hey, take it easy." She laughed nervously.

Just as he was about to dive on top of her, the land phone rang. Tim hurried into the kitchen.

"Where are you going?"

"I have to answer the phone."

"Leave it."

After he answered the phone, he returned to the bedroom. "Some damn kid playing with the phone."

"Forget him," she smiled.

"Forget who?" he laughed, sliding into the bed on top of her.

"That's the spirit."

He pulled off his shirt and unbuttoned hers. "You smell delicious," he whispered into her ear. Then the phone rang again.

"Ignore it," she demanded.

"I can't." Tim walked quickly through the living room and into the kitchen. He answered, and once again, he heard a boy's voice asking him if his refrigerator was running. This time, he glanced at the caller ID and then took a better look. It was his brother's name. He quickly answered, "Hello."

"Hey, Sir, is your…."

"Hey, kid, where'd you get that phone?"

There was silence for a few seconds, and then the caller continued, "Is your refrigerator running?" A small chuckle sounded.

"Kid, I'll buy that cell phone from you for three hundred dollars."

"What?"

"I'll give you three hundred dollars for the phone you're using. Where can I meet you?"

There was silence and then whispering. Now, a different kid's voice that sounded older asked, "Why do you want the phone?"

"I have caller ID, and that phone belongs to a friend of mine. He promised to sell it to me, but he lost it. Looks like you were the lucky person who found it, so I'll buy it from you instead."

This time there was a longer pause and more whispering. "I'm at Johnsons Park by the slide."

"What city?"

"Romulus."

"What time?"

There was more whispering. "I'm here now, but I'm leaving in an hour."

"I'm on my way. Oh, and kid, quit calling people on that phone."

"Tony, I'm waiting!"

He rushed into the bedroom. "Susan, I mean Sandy. That was Robin. She's on her way back. You've got to get out of here."

"Who's Susan?"

"I messed up your name that's all."

"That's all! I'd say that's enough. Why do I have to go? She knows about us now. What about the divorce? What happened to that?"

"I don't know. I just…you have to go…I don't have time for this."

"This? This is me. You don't have time for me? Are you staying with her or what? You need to make up your mind." She buttoned up her shirt. "It's me or it's her!"

He ran his hands roughly through his hair. "I can't right now."

"Well, it better be soon." She stormed out of the apartment slamming the door.

"Wait," he called out and ran to the door, flung it open, and saw Jill standing there. "What do you want?" he asked irritably.

Jill glanced down the hall and saw the back of Sandy who was turning the corner and heading down the stairs. "Nothing, I'm just walking to my apartment."

Tim slammed the door, marched to the spare room, and punched a hole in the wall with his fist. He mumbled, "I'll kill that nosey broad." After a few moments in which his anger subsided, he seated himself at the computer and searched online for directions to Johnsons Park.

When he found what he needed, he waited in the living room for Robin. As soon as she entered the apartment, he grabbed her by the arm and guided her out.

She had a handful of mail. "What's going on?"

"We have to go and get something."

"What? Wait, I have to tell you something."

"Tell me in the truck." He locked the door and pulled it shut. Then he saw Jill step out into the hall. "Figures," he mumbled.

Tim pulled Robin down the hall, walking quickly past Jill. "Hurry."

"Ouch! You're hurting me."

"Walk faster then."

"How is your nephew?" Jill's voice rang out as she ran to catch up to them.

Tim gripped tighter onto Robin. "Jen, Jill, whatever your name is, we're busy."

"I just wanted to know how your nephew was doing," she said as she moved in front of them.

"He's fine." Tim stepped around her and pulled Robin with him.

Jill followed them to the parking lot. "Bye."

Tim watched her enter her white Taurus. "I hate her," he mumbled.

"She's just trying to be friendly."

"Shut up."

Tim shoved Robin towards the passenger door. "Hurry, get in."

After he quickly entered the truck on the driver's side, he started the engine and sped to the highway. When he looked in his rearview mirror, he saw Jill's car. "That nosey bitch is following us."

"She's probably just going somewhere. It's the expressway. Everyone uses it."

When he exited the highway, the white Taurus was still behind him. "I'm going to lose her," he stated and then took a couple quick lane passes in and out of traffic, then a quick turn down one street, and an even quicker turn down another.

"Mission accomplished," he grinned. He pulled the internet map from his pocket, unfolded it, and handed it to Robin. "Where are we?"

"Where are we going?"

"To the park on that map. Which street is this?"

Robin read the street sign. "Goddard."

"Which way do I turn?"

"Why are we going here?"

"Which way?"

"Right."

He turned. "What was your news that you wanted to tell me?"

"Why are we going here?"

"What was your news?" he demanded.

"A boy called me from Tony's cell phone."

"The kid called the apartment, too."

"How did he get Tony's phone?"

"I don't know, but I'm going to find out. What's my next turn?"

She dropped the mail on the center console and focused on the map. "Are you going after the boy?"

"We are. The boy's going to sell me the phone. Which way, left?"

"Right. How will that help?"

"I'll question the kid. I'll find out who gave him the phone. Then we'll know who has Tony's body. Which way now?"

"Um…um."

"Which way?" he shouted.

"Turn around."

"What?"

"You went the wrong way."

"You said to go right."

"No, you said left, and I said that you were right. You know, right about going left."

"Give me the damn map." He ripped it from her hands. He studied it for a second and then shoved it back at her. "Learn to read a map."

Once he turned the truck around and had traveled down two more roads, he asked, "Left?"

"Left," she agreed.

"He turned and pulled the SUV off the road and onto a long, dirt drive that led to a park surrounded by woods. There were two empty baseball fields, a brick restroom, and a play area. There was a backhoe and three large, cement, sewer pipes near the swings and the slide.

"I don't see anyone," Robin commented.

He parked but kept the truck running. "You stay here." Tim got out, hustled over to the large slide, and stood behind it, waiting.

CHAPTER 26

No Deal

Billy Dobbs and his brother Jeff were hiding inside of a cylinder, concrete, sewer pipe. One opening slightly faced the slide. They saw the man, and Jeff giggled. "There he is."

"Shh. Stay back," Billy whispered.

"Aren't you going to sell him the phone?"

"No. I told you that if he looked scary, we wouldn't, and he looks mean."

"What are we going to do?"

"Wait until he leaves and then go home."

Three minutes went by. The man was now sitting on the end of the slide. His face wore an angry expression.

Jeff whispered, "What if he doesn't leave?"

"He will. He can't stay there forever."

"You'll miss your baseball game."

"No, I won't. Give me the phone, Jeff."

"No. I'm calling Dad."

"No!"

The man walked over to the swings, glanced out at the woods behind them, and grabbed onto the metal, chain link fence. He shook it, making a rattling sound. "Hey, kid, where are you? A deal is a deal. Come on out and give me that phone. I've got your money." Then he walked over to the sewer pipe near the swings and looked inside. Now, he was heading toward the next cement cylinder.

"He's going to find us," Jeff said, sounding scared. "I'm calling Dad."

"No. We're going to run. When I count to…"

Jeff took off running toward the opening of the park. He ran as fast as he could.

Billy froze in terror, watching and listening to his younger brother scream as the man grabbed him.

"Daddy! Daddy!" The cell phone dropped out of Jeff's hand.

Billy helplessly watched as the man picked it up and stuffed it into his pocket. The man covered Jeff's mouth with his right hand, wrapped his left arm around his waist, and picked him up. The stranger carried his brother to the back of an old, green SUV and shoved him into the back seat. He then crawled in beside Jeff. Billy heard the man yell, "Robin, scoot over and drive!"

Billy saw a woman move from the front passenger seat to the driver's seat. Then she threw a couple of papers out the driver's window. Now, she was looking straight at him. He watched the truck leave the park, and then he ran over to the papers. One was a map made from the internet and the other was a phone bill.

CHAPTER 27

Lost

Tim was preoccupied with the struggling boy while Robin was driving. He didn't pay much attention to her beyond yelling at her to slow down.

Robin was driving sporadically while trying to watch Tim and the scared child in the back seat. She saw Tim tying his arms and legs with rope.

When he was finished, he looked out the window. "Why aren't we on the highway yet?"

"I'm lost."

"Where's the map?"

"I don't know."

"Look for it."

"I did. I think it blew out the window."

"You're an idiot." Tim noticed that they were in an isolated area: very woodsy and no buildings in sight. "Pull over."

"Where?"

"Here."

She pulled the truck over to the side of the dirt road and parked. "I think I just turned too soon on that one road."

"Get back here with the kid."

She hurried out of the truck. Without hesitation, she climbed in back with the boy. "Things will be all right," she said, patting him softly on his arm.

Taking the keys with him, Tim exited the truck and started walking toward a few large piles of dirt about twenty feet away. "I'm going to take a piss. Stay here."

After he was done with his personal business, he noticed that the piles of dirt were next to a large hole, a cemented one. He looked around for construction vehicles, but there were none. It was as though someone had started to build a house and then abandoned the job.

While he was examining the basement, Robin walked up beside him. He jumped, "What are you doing? I said to stay in the truck."

"Why are you taking him? You have the phone."

"I want the body."

"So, ask him where it is and let him go."

"Who the hell are you all of a sudden?"

He was about to hit her, but she hurried away, moving quickly to the other side of the cement hole. "What is this, a basement?"

Tim yelled at her. "Stay here! Right, here," he demanded through clenched teeth. He ran back to the truck and grabbed the boy. He carried him to the basement and dangled him over it head first. "Tell me where you got the cell phone, and I'll let you go home."

"From my brother," he cried.

"Where is he?"

"The park."

"Where did he get the phone?"

"From my dad."

"Where did your dad get the phone?"

"I don't know."

Tim threw the boy up into the air over the ten-foot drop, and he let him fall a short distance just before he caught him. "The next time, I'm not going to catch you, and you are going to fall on your head. Splat," he shouted.

"I don't know. I don't know," the boy cried.

"Stop it!" Robin screamed. "He doesn't know. Please, just let him go."

Tim set him on the ground. "If his father wants him back, he'll give me what is mine."

CHAPTER 28

Missing Cell Phone

John Dobbs had just finished showering when he heard his daughter yell, "Dad, the phone's for you."

"Okay, I'll be there in a minute," he called through the door. Quickly, he toweled off and dressed into a pair of jeans and a tee shirt. John hurried to the phone.

"Hey John, it's me. Did you get anything from the cell phone?" Hall asked.

"I tried to use it when I got home, but the battery was dead, and it had to recharge. I'll call you back as soon as I check the phone numbers on it."

"I'm not far away."

"Sure, come on over."

John Dobbs hung up the phone and walked into the living room. His fourteen-year old daughter, Taylor, was watching a movie. He stepped in front of the screen. "Good morning."

"It's afternoon, Dad. Move over."

"Where's your mother?"

"I don't know."

"Oh." He walked over to the end table and saw the charger cord. "Where's the cell phone that was hooked to this?"

"I don't know."

"What time did you get up?"

"About twenty minutes ago."

He walked to the boys' bedroom and looked in. Then he returned to the living room and stood in front of the television. "Where's your brothers?"

"I don't know. Dad! I'm trying to watch this."

John walked into the kitchen, picked up the land phone, and pushed the numbers for his wife's cell phone. He poured himself a bowl of cereal while he waited.

"Hello."

"Where are you?"

"The grocery store. Do you need me to pick something up?"

"Honey, I used your charger to charge a cell phone that I brought home this morning."

"I wondered why my charger was in the living room."

"Where's the cell phone?"

"I didn't see one."

"Will you ask the boys if they took it?"

"How will I do that?"

"Aren't they with you?"

"No, but I know where they are. They asked to go to the park this morning, and I said that they could as long as Taylor went with them."

"Taylor just woke up, and the boys are gone."

"I'll ground them both when I get home."

"I'll go to the park and get them."

He got off the phone with his wife. "Taylor, I'm going to go get your brothers."

"Dad, you don't have to stand in front of the TV to talk to me."

"Then, answer me, so I know you heard me."

"Okay."

He started to leave, but his partner was at the door. "Hey, John."

"What are you doing in your uniform?"

"Investigating."

"It's our day off."

"Yeah, I know."

"Are you bucking for a promotion or something?"

"No, I just want to solve this case."

"Hey, um, slight problem. My knuckle headed boys took the cell phone down to the park. I'm going after them right now."

"I'll drive," Mark offered.

John walked to the passenger side of the police car. "How are they going to prep this car for us tomorrow if you're parading around in it today?"

"I'll take it to the station after this. Where to?"

"Johnsons Park."

Mark slowed down to let a squirrel cross the street. "I hope they don't erase any of the numbers on it. The last call the victim made could be a major clue to finding out what happened to him."

"Yeah, I know," John said, sounding guilty.

"How are we going to alert his relatives or find out who he even is?"

"I know. I'm sorry. Don't worry. The boys have it, and they probably just called their friends on it. We'll get it back."

"The owner of the Escort was a young girl. I don't think she had anything to do with it. Her father didn't want her to talk to me, but I did get a couple of names from her. She said that two boys gave her and two of her friends a ride.

They were traveling in a green SUV. We could question them later."

"You should give your information to the crime unit. Let them investigate it. It's not our job, and besides, Billy has a baseball game today. I thought you wanted to come."

"I do, but I really want to crack this case."

"You're a workaholic?"

"No, I'm not." He paused for a moment. "Oh, I went to the hospital."

"Did he live?"

"Yeah, but he's a mess. His mouth is wired shut. He's got so many casts, he looks like a mummy. I couldn't even get a fingerprint."

"Question him, and have him blink his answers."

"No, he's on a morphine drip: pretty much out of his mind. Besides, one eye's bandaged and the other one is swelled."

"I'm surprised he lived."

Mark drove into the park. "I don't see anyone here."

"Maybe we missed them. They might have taken the shortcut through the woods. When I was a kid, I'd always jump that fence," he said while looking at the fence behind the swings, "and I'd cut through the woods. That's probably what they did. They took the short cut home, and we missed them. They're probably back at the house."

John used his cell phone and called home. Taylor told him that the boys were not back yet. John and his partner examined the playground.

"Mark, drive out to the road on the other side of the park. Wait for me. I'm going to jump the fence and cut through the woods."

It had been awhile since he had climbed a fence. His landing was not as smooth as he had hoped. After regaining his balance, John took note of his surroundings. The woods smelled fresh. Several birds whistled, and two chipmunks scurried through the grass and climbed up the distant trees. As John walked on a thin trail that led to the road, he spied a squirrel darting from one tree to another. Then something up ahead scared it, and the animal ran off. As John continued walking through the woods, he heard crying and ran toward the noise. There, on the ground, curled up in front of a large oak tree, was his oldest son.

Billy looked up at his father through teary eyes. "He's gone. I can't find Jeff."

"What happened, Billy?"

"I don't know."

John helped him up. "Tell me what happened." He almost shook his son. "Where's your brother? Where is he?"

"I don't know, Dad. We were playing hide-and-seek and…"

"Where?"

"Here, in the woods."

"You were playing hide-and-seek in the woods?"

"Yeah."

"What happened?"

"It was Jeff's turn to hide, and I couldn't find him. I kept yelling for him, but he never answered." He started crying again.

"Who else was playing with you?"

"Just us."

"Okay, Son, calm down." Quickly, he ran to the road and Billy followed. "Mark," he yelled before reaching him. "Jeff's lost in the woods. Call it in and let's get a search party here. Son, go home. When your mom gets back from the store, tell her what's going on."

When Billy came in the door, his mother was already there. She was putting the groceries away. She glanced at him. "You better get washed up and put on your baseball uniform. After we eat, we're going to your game."

He remained by the doorway. "Mom, Dad is getting a search party to…" He choked up and ran off to his bedroom.

She closed the refrigerator door and ran after him. "What? A search party? Billy, what's wrong?"

Billy closed his door and locked it. "It's Jeff," he cried.

"Where's Jeff?"

He could hear the panic in his mother's voice. Feeling guilty and scared, he replied, "he's lost."

Taylor had seen her brother and mother run through the living room and down the hallway. She turned off the television and yelled, "What's going on?"

Mary Dobbs pulled on the doorknob. "Billy, unlock this door."

He couldn't. His mother was not like his father. She could tell when he was lying.

CHAPTER 29

Missing Child

John sat down on the couch beside his wife and hugged her. "It's not your fault. They didn't wait for Taylor like they were supposed to."

"I just keep picturing him hurt and scared." She cried.

"The helicopter is going to fly over, and I'm sure they'll spot him."

"A wild dog could have attacked him. Those woods are full of them."

"He'll be fine. We'll find him."

"I just never thought of them jumping the fence and playing in the woods. I just didn't think. I mean, they're kids, of course, they're going to do stuff like that."

"It's not your fault. Have something to eat. Rest up, so we can check the woods again. I think the search party missed a couple areas."

"Okay," she said sounding hopeful.

There was a knock at the door. John saw that it was his partner. He stepped out of the house.

Hall saw the anticipation in John's eyes. "Nothing yet," he said quickly. "The pilot is on his way. John, I'm sure he'll be able to spot him. Hang in there, buddy."

"It just seems like if he were there, we would have found him by now."

"Did you ask Billy about the cell phone?"

"No," he scowled. "There's more important things going on right now, don't you think? My son is missing. I don't care about a damn cell phone."

Hall looked apologetic. "Sorry." He turned and walked away.

Billy watched out his bedroom window. He had heard Officer Hall ask his father about the cell phone, and he was relieved that his dad did not want to deal with it. If he had only known ahead of time the trouble that cell phone was going to cause him and his family, he never would have touched it. He heard his mother crying in the living room, and he promised himself that he would fix everything.

Billy waited for the right time. It took until 6:00 p.m. before his parents finally left him and his sister alone at the house. She was babysitting him. He hated that terminology. Why couldn't they call it something else: something more dignified? After all, he was eleven, almost twelve. He walked to Taylor's bedroom and tapped lightly on her door. "Taylor?"

She opened the door. "Billy, Mom wants you to eat something."

"When will they be back?"

"I don't know. They're searching the woods again."

"I'm going to make a sandwich."

"Do you want me to make one for you?"

"No," he said quickly and then added, "You look tired. I'll do it."

Billy saw that she, too, like his mother, had been crying. Her eyes were swollen and puffy. The guilt he felt was insurmountable. He had hurt his whole family.

After she closed her door, he ran to the kitchen, scooted a chair next to the refrigerator, and stood on it. Opening the cupboard door, he carefully reached in and removed the gun case and the key from the coffee cup. Quietly, he closed the cabinet door, climbed down from the chair, and hurried back to his bedroom.

He sat on his brother's bed. Slowly, he unlocked the box and pulled out his dad's 9mm Glock and an empty magazine. Billy knew his father kept the loaded magazine somewhere else as a safety measure. His parents had discussed it one morning during one of their grown up talks. Not ever having intended on using his father's weapon for real, Billy never cared to know where his father kept that loaded magazine. As he stared at the empty magazine, he now wished he knew. Then, he saw a small box inside the gun case. He read the word Winchester on it. Nervously, he opened it and dumped the contents onto the bed. Six bullets fell out. He pushed each bullet into the magazine, and then Billy shoved the magazine securely into the bottom of the pistol until he heard a metallic clank sound.

After returning the gun case and the key to the cupboard, Billy ran to his bedroom. He wrapped the gun with his white baseball shirt and placed it into his orange backpack. He checked his front pocket to make sure that he had the paper with the directions and the phone bill with the address on it, and then he grabbed his wallet off his dresser and stuck it in his back pocket.

Billy was afraid to face the man, but he was more fearful of how his Mom, Dad, and sister would hate him once they knew that Jeff's disappearance was his fault. He left quietly, sneaking out to the garage to get his bicycle. Quickly, he rode to the taxicab company in town.

CHAPTER 30

Patient

The drugs were wonderful. He couldn't feel a thing. Tony didn't care about anything either. Lying in his hospital bed with several I.V. cords plugged into him, he thought of nothing important as he listened to the slow beating of his heart: thud......, thud.........., thud..............., thud................ It seemed to be slowing down as he drifted in and out of a sleepy haze.

A nurse entered. She unhooked something down by his bedside: a large plastic bag full of his urine. Tony smiled in his mind. The lady dressed in pink pajamas emptied the bag in the bathroom and hooked it back up again. Then, she changed the bag on his I.V. stand. "Are you awake?"

Tony's face was bandaged and swollen, and his jaw wired shut. There was no way that he could form a smile with his cheeks or lips. The best he could do was try to communicate through his mind, so again he smiled on the inside. His one good, yet swollen eye followed her unintelligibly. She was nothing more than an object to exercise his vision.

When he awoke hours later, he was alone. He felt throbbing sharp pains in his head and in his chest, ribs, foot, leg, arms, eye, and jaw. Even his eyelashes hurt. Sheer pain was all he could feel, and he wanted to scream. Where's the woman in the pajamas? Where is a doctor, a nurse, anyone? Help, he wanted to yell out, but his mouth would not open. Out of his right eye, he saw a cord with a little button on the end of it. This had to be the call button for the nurse. Tony tried to push his right arm forward: the one arm that remained in working condition while he had endured his misery in the bag, but as he flung it forward, he discovered that his right hand was in an enclosed cast just like his left hand. His left arm was in a cast as well. Maybe I can kick one of these wires lose and someone will come and help me, he thought. His good eye focused past the cast on his right foot and over to his left leg. He sighed relief at seeing his actual leg, but as his eye traveled to the end of it, there was a cast on his left foot. That was it. He was at the mercy of others. Helplessly, he suffered in his anguishing pain. Tears found their way out of the one swollen eye that still worked.

What happened to me? Who did this to me? A flash of memory showed itself, and he saw his brother hitting him in the kitchen of his own apartment. It was my brother. My very own flesh and blood did this to me. Why? Was it to take Robin from me? Did she hate me this much? Why did she let him in the apartment? Was it the two of them together?

Please, someone, come in. God, please send someone into my room. Lord, please, I'm in so much pain. I can't take it. Hit me with a lightening bolt and get it over with. Please!

It seemed like days had gone by, but it had only been minutes. A nurse stepped in and pushed a button on a box. Aaah, yes! Almost instantly, his mind stopped asking questions and the physical pain dulled as he returned to the hazy state where nothing mattered, and the only sound he paid attention to was the soft thud of his heart slowly beating.

The nurse removed the bandage wrapped around his head and part of his face. "I'm going to put a new bandage on you. Wow, you kind of look like my brother-in-law, Tony."

He gazed up at the woman who was now just an amusing, pretty object. She wasn't the same one as before, but she had on the same kind of pajamas.

CHAPTER 31

Nosey Neighbor

It was 6:00 p.m., Sunday, and Robin paced back and forth in the living room. It pained her to see the small child scared and shaking on the couch. His little cheeks were still wet with tears. Already, he had a bruise across his forehead where Tim had slapped him.

Tim sat in the recliner chomping on potato chips and drinking a beer. "Robin, sit the hell down."

"He needs to go to the hospital."

"He's fine. I barely touched him."

"He hit his head when he fell."

"He's fine."

"People are going to be looking for him. We should let him go."

"Not until I get Tony's body back." Tim guzzled his beer.

"What if his father doesn't have it?"

Tim's hand tightened around the empty beer can, crushed it, and dropped it onto the floor. "He had the phone."

"What are you going to do?"

"Make an even trade," Tim said looking at the boy.

Robin's cell phone rang. She went into the bedroom to answer it. Tim followed her and stood by the door listening. She could see the shadow of his boots under the door. "It's my sister," she called out.

"So, talk to her out here."

Robin carried the phone into the living room. "Oh, that's too bad. Yes, I'll check on him. Sure. What is the emergency?"

"What's she saying?" Tim demanded.

"Yeah, that was Tony's voice. Hold on." Robin pulled the phone away from her ear and covered the mouthpiece. "Sharon's at the hospital. She was called in on an emergency, and she wants me to check on Craig for her."

As her sister told her about the emergency and the patient, Robin pressed the phone to her ear. There was a long pause while Robin absorbed the information: an ambulance delivered a man during the wee hours of the morning. Police officers had found him in a body bag in a ditch along the highway. He was so broken up that the doctors were not even sure if he would live. "Oh, yes!" Robin yelled out, unable to contain her happiness. God had answered her prayers. Her husband was alive. Her baby would have a father after all.

"What is it?" Tim demanded.

There was a knock at the apartment door. "Sis, I have to go. Someone's at the door."

Tim was already at the peephole. "It's that nosey broad from next door. You get rid of her," he warned. He picked the boy up and carried him into the bedroom while Robin opened the door.

Jill rushed in. Speaking fast, she said, "I saw you coming in. I hope you don't mind. I was just baking some cookies, and I ran out of eggs. It always happens that way. I'm sorry to bother you, but would you loan me an egg? I'd go to the store, but I'm right in the middle of making the cake."

"I thought it was cookies."

"Those, too."

"Sure, I'll give you an egg. Are you sure you only need one?"

"Yes, just one. Thanks."

Robin walked into the kitchen to get the egg, and for the first time, she noticed a television on the kitchen table. Quickly, she retrieved an egg from the refrigerator and headed back to the doorway, but Jill was now standing in the living room and seemed to be looking for something.

"Here's your egg," Robin said handing it to her.

"Thanks again. Um, I was looking out my window earlier today, and I saw you and Tony coming into the apartment, and you had a boy with you."

Robin walked to the apartment door in a hurry. "Relative."

Jill followed her slowly. "I couldn't help but see that he was crying."

"You know kids. They don't like to hear the word no."

"Some cookies would cheer him up. Would it be all right if I…"

"He's diabetic."

"Oh."

"I hope your cookies and cake turn out fine. Bye." She held the door open.

"Thanks," Jill said and remained standing near the doorway. "Robin," she whispered, "earlier today, I saw that redheaded friend of Tony's leaving your apartment. I don't want to get involved in your business or anything, but I think your husband is cheating on you."

Robin's mouth dropped open, and she stood still for a few seconds. It was as if her world had stopped. Now, that

Tony's alive, how will I stop him from seeing that girl? she thought.

"I'm sorry. Maybe I shouldn't have said anything."

"It's okay. I know about it," she whispered and stepped out of the apartment.

Jill followed her and sighed relief. "I didn't want to be the one to tell you. I hardly know you, but someone should tell you."

"I'm going to talk to the marriage counselor about it. Things will be all right," she assured Jill and herself.

Jill remained standing next to Robin. "Again, I don't want to pry, but I noticed some bruises on you."

"I fell. Bye." Robin quickly stepped back into her apartment and closed the door.

Tim rushed into the living room. "What did she want?"

"To borrow an egg."

"She's snooping around."

Before Robin could tell him her news, Tim walked back into the bedroom. Robin heard the boy crying for a second. She was about to rush to him, but Tim returned to the living room. He shoved the phone at Robin and a piece of paper with a telephone number on it. "It's the kid's phone number. Call it and get a meeting with his dad. Tell him we'll swap his kid for the body. If he doesn't want to, I'll kill his kid."

"His dad doesn't have the body."

"How do you know?"

"Tony's alive."

"No, he's not."

"Yes." She couldn't help it; she was smiling. "Sharon called to the hospital because of an emergency, and I guess they're short staffed and..."

"Get to it."

"She said that a guy was brought in that was all busted up."

"That could be anyone."

"The police found him in a body bag in a ditch off the highway."

Tim's face dropped. "What? No! He can't be alive. He was dead."

"This is good news. You can leave. I'll let the boy go a couple of streets away from his home, or...I know...I'll take him back to the park."

"You can't. That whole area will be crawling with cops. This isn't good news. I've been Tony already. People have seen me. My mother talked to me."

Robin hated to admit it, but he was right. He couldn't just leave. "I guess you'll have to stay and be him until he gets well enough to come home. Then, you can leave."

"That's right," he said, relaxing a bit. "There will still be the problem with him knowing what we did."

"What you did," she corrected him. "Maybe he won't remember."

"He'll know I took his identity. This isn't going to work. If I go to prison, you're going with me."

"We won't go to prison. I'll talk to Tony. I'll explain to him that we thought he was dead."

"That's not going to work."

She frowned, but then she gently touched her belly. "It will work."

"No. We are going to go to that hospital and identify Tony as me. Then, I'm going to kill him."

"No!"

"I'm staying Tony," the anger rose in his voice.

"He's at the hospital. You're not him."

After a long pause, he said, "It's prison or this, and I'm choosing this."

"Well, I'm not choosing either one. I want Tony back."

He examined her eyes for a second, walked over to her, and grabbed her chin in his right hand. Tim tilted her face up to meet her eyes with his. "Tony isn't going to suddenly love you again. Did you forget his girlfriend?"

"I don't care about her."

"Do you think Tony is going to forgive you for trying to kill him?"

"I didn't."

"You hired me to do it, and that's what I'm going to tell him."

"That's fine. Tell him what you want but let him live. I want you to leave."

Tim let her go, walked into the bedroom, and dragged the frightened boy out into the living room. "You want him dead?"

"No!"

"I'll kill him if you don't do what I say." He squeezed his hand around the boy's neck.

"Let him go."

Tim squeezed tighter. "I can't hear you."

"I'll do it. I'll do it!"

"Then, say it. Say that I'm Tony."

"You're Tony. You're Tony," she cried.

Tim released his grip. The boy collapsed onto the floor nearly unconscious.

Robin ran over to him and gently held him. Her mind agonized over her ignorance. *What was I thinking? Tim's a monster. I should have known he wouldn't be happy about the news of his brother.* She looked at the scared child in her arms and tried not to let her anger or fear reveal itself in her voice. "When are we going to let this boy go?"

"I'm going to let him go very soon, right over the top of that basement."

"No!"

"He seen us, and he knows too much."

"Please, he's just a boy. He doesn't even know where he's at. He won't be able to tell anyone much of anything."

There was a knock at the door. Tim looked through the peephole. He marched across the room and grabbed the boy. "You get rid of her and don't say anything to her. Don't think about stepping one foot out of this apartment either. I'm going to be right in there," he said pointing to the kitchen, "and if I hear you say anything that you shouldn't, I'll snap this kid's neck like a potato chip. You understand?"

She nodded her head and watched him carry the boy into the kitchen. Opening the apartment door, she forced a smile. "Do you need another egg?"

"Yes, I'm sorry."

Robin blocked the entrance, keeping Jill at the doorway. "Wait right here. I'll be right back." She briskly walked through the living room and into the kitchen. When Robin opened the refrigerator, she heard Jill's voice.

"Kittykay!" Jill called out. "Get back here!"

Immediately, Robin looked at Tim and saw the anger in his eyes. "I'll take care of it," she whispered. Robin grabbed the whole egg carton and ran out of the kitchen.

The cat sprinted through the living room and down the hallway. Jill ran after her. "Kittykay, come here."

Robin didn't chase after her right away, but instead she stayed in the living room, and called out, "I'll get your cat." In a desperate attempt to save the boy's life, she picked up an ink pen from the corner table and wrote on the inside of the egg carton. HELP! HE IS GOING TO KILL THE BOY IN BASEMENT IN WOODS NEAR PARK. She ran down the hallway.

Clearly, Jill saw the cat slip into the bathroom, but she shoved the bedroom door open wide. "Did you go in here, Kittykay?"

While she was snooping in the bedroom, Robin picked up the cat from the bathroom and ran after Jill. "Look, I found her. Here," Robin said anxiously, as she thrust the cat into Jill's arms.

"Thank you. Sorry about that," Jill said as she let Robin walk her to the door.

"Here, don't forget the egg," she said and placed the whole carton into Jill's one free hand.

"Thanks, but I only need one."

"I have another carton. Please, just take it."

"No, I only need one."

"That's okay. Please," she said almost begging.

Jill kept the carton in her hand. "Okay, thanks."

"Bye." Robin closed the door.

Tim stormed out of the kitchen. "That nosey broad is going to get it."

"She was just borrowing an egg. Neighbors do that."

"This morning, when she was poking her nose around here, she asked if my truck was mine or my brother's."

"How would she know to ask that?" Robin wondered aloud.

"My mother, that's how. Now, I have to ditch the truck."

Robin saw that the boy was shaking and crying. She just couldn't live with herself if Tim killed him. "Please, Tim, let him go. I'll take the blame for everything. I'll even say that I'm responsible for what happened to Tony. Please, leave."

"I'm not leaving, but I will change the plans."

She sighed relief, thinking that he had decided to let the boy live. Thank God, she thought the man does have some compassion.

He dropped the boy, reached out, and twisted her arms up behind her back. "You're going to have an accident, too." Tim smiled and added, "On your way to your mother's."

"Leave me alone. Let me go."

The struggle was not much from Robin's end. She was afraid that Tim would hurt her baby. After he tied her hands and feet together with rope, he said, "You're just one more problem." He smacked tape over her mouth and placed her and the boy into the bedroom closet.

The boy's muffled crying was louder now. Robin wished that she could at least save him. She thought about their chances. Maybe Jill was reading the message on the inside of the egg carton and talking with the police, or the boy at the park had found the map and piece of mail that she had thrown out the window of the truck. Perhaps, right now, he was talking with the police.

She heard knocking at the apartment door. Tim's voice was loud and stern. "No, we don't have any milk."

Now, she heard Jill's voice just as loud and stern as his, "May I talk with Robin?"

"No. She's sleeping. Don't knock on our door again." His voice rang out even louder than before. Then, there were the sounds of the door slamming and Tim's feet stomping their way into the bedroom.

Robin could now hear her own muffled cries of fear as she struggled against her binding ropes. There was the sound of keys clashing to the floor and Tim's footsteps stomping back down the hallway and then the apartment door slamming shut. Her body relaxed, but her mind continued to race, trying to think up an escape for the boy, herself, and her baby.

CHAPTER 32

Hospital Visit

Moving at a quick pace, Tim drove his SUV into the subdivision behind the apartment building. Even though it was an upscale neighborhood, there were several empty houses because of the mortgage crisis and failing businesses. Easily, he spied out three abandoned homes and chose the one that was most secluded. The glass on the side door to the garage was already broken out. He simply put his hand through the window, grabbed the knob, and opened the door. He lifted the garage door and shoved it up. Quickly, he drove his truck in, pulled down the garage door, and ran back to the parking lot where he slid into his brother's Avenger.

At 7:00 p.m., Tim arrived at the hospital. He walked confidently up to the nurses' station. "I need to speak with Sharon."

"Which Sharon?" the nurse asked.

He thought for a few seconds. "The one who has a son named Craig."

"Who are you?"

"Tony Henkeson, her brother-in-law."

The nurse paged Sharon and then told Tim to wait in the visitors' lounge. He walked down the hallway hoping to spot his brother's room on the way.

A few minutes later, Sharon appeared, but Tim continued to watch a small television screen in the waiting room. "Tony," she said surprised.

"Oh, Sharon. I'm here to see that guy you told Robin about."

"Really?"

"My twin brother, Tim, is missing. He was let out of prison a few weeks ago, and no one has seen him for a few days."

"Oh, that's too bad. I hope this isn't him though. This guy is pretty bad off."

"You mean he might die?"

"I'm afraid so. He's struggling just to breathe. You know, when I was changing his bandages, I thought he looked like you."

"Really?"

"Come with me. I'll show him to you." While they were heading to the room, she asked, "Are you excited about being a father?"

"What?"

"Oh, she didn't tell you yet?"

"No."

"Oh, please don't tell her I told you. I have such a big mouth. She wanted to surprise you on your anniversary night. I haven't had much sleep lately."

"Don't worry about it."

"Well, are you excited?"

"Oh yeah, I am." Now, he hated Robin even more.

"Robin said your mother was always bugging her about having children."

"She bugs everyone."

"Well, here we are." She stopped in front of the doorway.

Tim could here the monitors beeping. This will be easy, he thought. I'll just unplug a few things.

The police officer stood up from his chair, so now Tim could see him over the food cart in the hallway. "I'm Officer Kent. Anyone who comes to see this man, has to see me first. I've been assigned to his case."

"My wife's sister," he said, pointing to her, "said that this man was brought in this morning, and my brother's been missing, and so, I thought, you know, maybe it could be him."

"I hope not for your brother's sake. This man has a lot of serious injuries."

"Oh, that's too bad."

"He was badly beaten."

"Is it okay if I look at him?"

"Sure."

Sharon's pager went off. "I have to go. Bye, Tony." She hugged him lightly. "Kiss Robin for me. Let me know if this guy is your brother."

He followed the police officer into the room. It was Tony. Without a doubt, it was him. The parts of his face that weren't badly bruised, swollen, stitched, or covered, were enough to tell.

"Wow," the officer said after noticing the resemblance.

"It's my brother, Tim. We're twins." He let out a long sigh.

"Identical?"

"Yes."

"Do you want to talk to him or hold his…" Looking at the right cast on his hand that extended to his elbow and the left cast that covered his hand and continued up to his shoulder, he said, "I guess you can't hold either hand. You can touch him; just look for a place that's not bandaged or in a cast."

"Can he hear me?"

"Yes, he's not in a coma, but the morphine he's on spaces his mind out, so he won't understand you. And, of course, he can't talk to you; his jaw's wired shut. If he could communicate, that would make the detectives' job simpler. They are trying to find out who did this to him. Do you know anyone who would want to hurt your brother?"

"I'm sure a lot of people. He has been nothing but bad news, in and out of prison a lot. He just got back out a few weeks ago. He was living with our mother."

"Sponging off of her?"

"I think he was going to get a job. After all, he did just get out of prison."

Officer Kent pulled out his notebook. "What is his full name?"

"Tim Eugene Henkerson."

"So, he didn't work. Any friends?"

"I don't know."

"What's your mother's phone number and address? She'll probably be able to answer some important questions. I'm sure she'll be glad to know her son's alive. Say, maybe, you'd rather be the first to tell her that you found your brother."

"No."

"Oh?"

"I mean, yes. Um, could I have a few minutes with him alone?"

"No, sorry." Officer Kent began to write again on his notebook. "What is your mother's phone number and address?"

Tim answered all of the officer's questions. Then a doctor entered the room. "You are family?"

"Yes, I'm his brother."

"Did you talk with the nurse?"

"Sort of."

"I'm Dr. Pia." He reached out to shake hands.

"Tony." He shook his hand half-heartedly. "Well, I really have to get…"

"Your brother is going to need a kidney in order to live. I'm sure you want to…"

"A what?"

"A kidney. People live fine with just one. Family is the best place to find donors."

Officer Kent interjected, "They're identical twins. What luck, huh?"

"Oh that is good news. Right now, your brother is recovering from many injuries, but he needs this kidney and soon. Will you be willing to have blood drawn for tests today? As soon as possible, we should operate. His chances of surviving will be much greater if he has this kidney."

"Of course, I want to help my brother. Um, it's just, I have some things to do. How long does he have?"

"Once he heals, as long a life as anyone his age."

"No, I mean if he doesn't get the kidney?"

The doctor looked worried. "I'm afraid, without the kidney, we are looking at possibly only days."

"Really?" Tim almost smiled but caught himself. "That's too bad."

"But, there is you, a perfect match. You being a twin, you can save your brother's life."

"I'll be back as soon as I can."

"Let me get a nurse to give you some forms to complete. That will move the process along quicker."

"Sure, okay."

Once Tim had the forms, he hurried down the hallway to leave. He saw Sharon. Pretending not to notice her, he tried to turn quickly around the corner.

She ran after him and touched his sleeve. "Tony, was it him?"

He stopped. "Yes, it was."

"Odd, I never met him."

"Well, he's been in prison for a while."

"My sister mentioned that you had a twin, but out of sight out of mind. Anyway, did you get to talk to one of his doctors?"

"Yes, I did." He started to walk away from her. "I have to go, so I can't talk right now."

She walked with him. "Tony, just a quick question."

He stopped. "Okay."

"Robin told me about her accident at work. Those bruises looked serious. I tried to tell her to see a doctor. She didn't want to. Now, that you know about the baby - thanks to my big mouth - you'll push her to make an appointment?"

"You bet I will."

"I'm sorry I ruined your surprise."

"You didn't ruin anything."

"Robin is going to hate me for telling you."

"I won't tell her."

"Oh, this morning, she almost passed out. I'm worried about her. She doesn't look healthy. I know some very good obstetricians. Perhaps you could convince her to switch doctors."

"I'll try."

Sharon's pager went off, and Tim looked relieved. Quickly, he took the opportunity to flee. When he reached the parking lot, he tossed the medical forms into a nearby trashcan.

CHAPTER 33

The Visitor

Billy Dobbs paid the cab driver and watched him drive away. He looked up at the building and removed the phone bill from his pocket. "Robin Hen-ker-son," he read her name. "Apartment 2A," he whispered to himself, and then he pulled on the building door and discovered it was locked. He sat down on the porch steps.

About ten minutes later, a car pulled into the handicap space near the door, and an elderly man stepped out. He opened the trunk and pulled out a wheelchair and a suitcase.

Billy saw him struggling. "Would you like some help, Mister?"

Fred Greenway jumped a bit. "Wow, where'd you come from?"

"I was sitting on the step."

"Who are you?"

Billy had already picked up the suitcase and was heading to the building door with it. Mr. Greenway opened the wheelchair and wheeled it over to his wife. He unfastened her seatbelt and helped her into the chair. As he did, she laughed, and Fred knew that her medicine was working. He tried to push the wheelchair up the ramp, but the brakes were stuck. Billy left the suitcase on the step and helped loosen the brake handle. Fred Greenway was pleased with the boy's unexpected help. Soon, they were in the apartment.

Edna cried when she saw Charlie on the floor. "He's dead!"

"No, he'll be all right." Fred picked up the ivy and handed it to Billy. "Could you hold this for a second?" Then he walked to the cupboard and pulled out a plastic container. Billy gently placed the plant inside. The two scooped up as much dirt as they could and repacked the plant. Fred watered it and placed it back on the end table. He wheeled Edna into her bedroom.

"Mister, I have to go," Billy called out as he left the apartment.

Fred heard the boy leave. Once he had Edna tucked safely into bed, he inspected the apartment. Many of their personal belongings looked out of place. He soon discovered that their television was missing. This was his and Edna's only source of entertainment since her illness. Now, he thought about their emergency money. Quietly, Fred crept into the bedroom. Carefully, he slid his hand in between the mattress and the box spring. Feeling nothing, he gave up his search. As Fred was stepping out of the bedroom, he saw his black sock on the floor near the disheveled shoeboxes. He picked it up and sadly shook his head.

Moments later, after watching Edna sink into a deeper sleep, Fred quietly snuck out of the apartment and walked to the Henkersons' and was surprised to see the boy who had helped him.

"What are you doing here?" Fred asked.

"I'm waiting."

"So, you know Tony and Robin Henkerson?"

"Yeah."

Fred saw Laura Knight coming down the hallway. "Hello," he said.

She smiled. "Hello, Mr. Greenway." Laura continued walking to her apartment. Just before entering, she looked again at her neighbor. "Are you waiting for the Henkersons?"

"We are."

"Would you like to wait in my apartment?"

"Sure." He smiled and followed her inside. Billy followed behind him.

Laura invited them to sit at the kitchen table. She offered them something to drink, and they both chose water. While she filled their glasses, she asked, "How is Edna?"

"Better. The doctors finally found some pain medicine that works."

She handed Fred his water. "That's good." As she handed Billy his water, she asked, "What's your name?"

"Billy."

"Fred, I didn't know you had any grandsons." She smiled.

"I don't. He's my new friend. He helped me bring Edna into the apartment. It's nice to meet young boys who have manners."

"Where are you from, Billy?" she asked.

"I live in the neighborhood," he answered with his head lowered and his eyes on the floor.

"Can't believe this economy, can you?" Fred asked.

Laura shook her head. "I know. It's scary. Just think, we used to talk about Michigan's crazy weather, and now all people talk about is the bad economy."

"Crime's up, too. Someone robbed Edna and me."

"Where?"

"Here."

"When?"

"While we were at the hospital this morning, someone took our television and our money."

"Oh, my gosh."

"That's what I want to talk to Tony about. He locked our place up for us. Maybe, he didn't pull the door shut all the way."

"Still, no one can get in this apartment building without a key. That means it was one of the other tenants. Did you call the police?"

"Not yet. I didn't want to upset Edna." Fred drank all of his water and set the empty glass on the counter. "I had better head back downstairs and check on Edna. I don't like to be away from her too long. Billy, maybe you could come down and let me know when Tony Henkerson arrives home?"

"Sure." Billy answered quickly.

"Sorry to hear you were robbed. Tell Edna hello for me."

"I will. Be careful to lock your door. Bye."

After Fred Greenway left, Laura realized she was now alone in her apartment with a stranger, and the more she examined him, the more uneasy she felt. The boy appeared tense and nervous as though something were wrong. He kept fidgeting and playing around with something in his backpack. Twice he had wiped sweat from his forehead. Kittykay entered the hallway. "Oh, look, here's my cat. She must have been sleeping. Usually, she greets me at the door."

Billy left his chair and sat on the floor. He reached out and petted the cat. "I love cats."

"How do you know the Henkersons?"

He stopped petting Kittykay and quickly stood up. "I'm going to go and try their door again. Thanks for the water. Bye," he said as he picked up his orange backpack and left.

She followed him, stood by the doorway, and watched him knock on the Henkersons' door. When no one answered, he walked over to the side of the wall, slid his back down it, and sat on the carpet, waiting. Laura thought about inviting him back inside, but he was a stranger, so she closed the door and locked it. Then she walked into the kitchen.

Moments later, Laura heard some commotion in the hallway. It sounded like people wrestling and bumping into the walls. She ran to the living room and peeked through the peephole. There was no one there. Cautiously, she opened the door, peered out, and searched right and then left. The hallway was empty. Billy was gone.

Laura thought about knocking on the Henkersons' door but reminded herself that this was none of her business, but the more she tried to subdue the desire to find out where Billy went, the more agitated she felt. Finally, she gave in to her concerns for the boy and knocked on the Henkersons' door. When there was no answer, she assuaged her worry with the thought that a tenant dropped groceries or something in the hallway, and Billy had simply left.

Ten minutes later, Laura was leaving her apartment when she ran into a middle-aged woman who was knocking on the Henkersons' door. Quickly, she tried to slip down the hallway unnoticed.

"Please, I need some help." Lilly Henkerson ran to her and took hold of her shoulder. "My son, Tim, is in the hospital, and he needs a kidney."

"A kidney?"

"The doctors are saying that he'll die if he doesn't get one."

"Well, that is awful." Beyond saying that, Laura did not know what more this frantic mother wanted her to do. "I'm sorry," she added and shifted her bag of clothing to her other arm.

Lilly Henkerson sounded desperate. "Tony could give him a kidney. I just can't get a hold of him though."

"Do you want me to give him a message if I see him?" Laura asked.

"No, he already knows. The doctor told me he was at the hospital earlier. I need to use your phone."

They entered Laura's apartment. Lilly Henkerson helped herself to the phone. When no one answered her call, she asked, "Where's Jill?"

"I'm not sure."

"She's very nice."

"I'll tell her you said so."

"She told me that she was apartment sitting."

"Yes, she's taking care of my cat. I'm Laura."

"I'm Lilly."

Laura stood in her living room waiting to leave. She picked up her bag of clothes again and looked at Lilly who had a determined look on her face as she pressed the receiver hard against her ear.

"If I don't get Tony to pick up, do you mind if I try to call his wife's cell number?"

"No," she set her bag of clothes down and took a seat in the recliner. Kittykay leaped onto her lap. Laura petted her cat and watched out the window for Jill while she listened to Lilly.

CHAPTER 34

The Dobbs Discovery

Officer John Dobbs and his wife entered the house slowly. They had never been this depressed, scared, and worried in their lives. Taylor ran into the living room. "Did you find Jeff?"

"No," her mother shook her head and cried.

"Don't give up hope." John hugged his wife. "We'll find him."

"Taylor, honey, help your mother to bed."

"I can't sleep," Mary protested.

"It won't do you any good to be overtired. We're going back out tonight and search the woods again."

She nodded her head and let her daughter guide her down the hallway. John followed behind them. He passed them and headed to Billy's bedroom. "Son," he called out, turning on the light. John turned quickly and headed back toward his wife and daughter. "Taylor, where's Billy?"

"I thought he was in his bedroom."

"He's not."

"Maybe he's in the basement."

"Right," John realized now that he was sounding paranoid. "Of course." He walked to the basement, switched on a light, and scanned the little recreation area that he and his wife had fixed up for their children. "Billy," he called out and continued to call as he walked through the house.

His wife and daughter met him in the living room. "Is he missing, too?" Taylor asked frantically.

"What?" His wife cried.

"Calm down. He probably went to a friend's house. Let me make a few phone calls." John entered the kitchen to get the phone book, and that is when he noticed that a kitchen chair was up next to the refrigerator. Answering his fearful question, he moved the chair away, opened the cupboard, and reached for his gun case. It felt light. He pulled the key from the cup and opened the case. It was empty. He ran to his bedroom and looked on the shelf above the closet rack. His loaded magazine was there.

His wife and daughter witnessed his frantic search. "What are you looking for, Dad?"

"Did your brother say anything about going somewhere?"

"No. He said that he was going to make a sandwich. Why? What's wrong?"

"Where is he, John?" his wife asked worried.

"Did he say anything else?"

"No, Dad."

"John, what is it?" his wife demanded, and when he didn't answer her, she quickly walked out of the bedroom and into the boys' room. "Billy," she called out. Not finding him, she headed into the living room. "Billy!"

"Mary," John chased after her, "he's gone."

Taylor followed her parents into the living room. "Where did he go?"

"I think he went to find Jeff." He hugged his wife. "I'll go get him. He couldn't have gone far."

"I'm going, too," Mary stated.

"You and Taylor drive around the neighborhood, and I'll go up to the park. Mary, he has my gun."

"What?" she cried in disbelief.

"It doesn't have any bullets in it," he assured her.

"Why would he take your gun?" Taylor asked.

"I don't know. Let's go," John said frustrated. Something was bothering him about the gun. Before he left, he checked the gun case again and saw the empty Winchester box. He knew that it had bullets in it. Now, he recalled that last week at the firing range, he had six bullets left in that box.

Mary ran to the garage to get into her minivan. Taylor followed. "Mom, his bike's missing."

"Go tell your father before he leaves."

Officer Mark Hall parked in the driveway and unknowingly blocked the minivan. Mary exited her vehicle and quickly approached him as he opened the door. "Did you find him?"

"No, I'm sorry. I need to talk to John."

"Billy's missing, too."

"What?"

"He took John's gun. We think that he went to look for his brother."

"Billy's got his father's gun?" he said in disbelief.

With relief in her voice, Mary stated, "It's not loaded. John, keeps the ammunition for it in a separate hiding place."

"I'll call the news station and have him added to the AMBER Alert."

"You don't think we'll find him? He's probably at the park or on one of the nearby streets. He's on his bike," she explained.

"Describe his bike for me," Mark said pulling out his notebook and pen.

While she was describing it, John and Taylor walked up. "Did they…" John began to ask.

"No," Mark answered quickly. "I'm going to add Billy to the AMBER Alert."

"He couldn't be too far." John said.

"Well, at least the gun's not loaded," Mark commented.

John pulled him over to the side, so his wife and daughter would not hear him. "It has six bullets in it. It was what I had left over from practice last week. I left the bullets in the case with my gun. I never do that," he said angry with himself. "I never leave the ammunition with the gun."

"John, I know you don't want me to talk about the cell phone, but there might be a link here," his partner explained.

"A link to what?"

"That guy's cell phone. What if…"

"What?" he raised his voice. Mary and Taylor heard him and walked over to them.

"Just hear me out," Mark pleaded.

"No, my boys are missing. I don't have time…"

"What if your sons phoned the killer on that phone? Think about it. The person who injured that guy, meant to kill him, probably thought that he was dead. Now, this murderer gets a phone call from two kids on a phone that should be in the dead victim's pocket. Now, that is going to piss someone off."

John's wife looked at her husband accusingly. "You brought a cell phone home that could get our sons killed?"

"No!"

"Why's Mark saying this?" she cried.

"He's speculating."

"No, I'm not. I already called Detective Nettle and linked your son, Jeff, to that case," Mark said.

John shook his head. "Oh, God, I can't believe this." He shook his head again, frustrated.

"Let's find Billy. Mary, you and Taylor drive around the block. John and I will drive into town and question people."

CHAPTER 35

The Plan

Tim waited for Sandy to arrive. When he had phoned her earlier, she had believed him about Robin granting him a divorce and leaving for her mother's to vacation in Tennessee. That's when she told him that their plan, hers and Tony's, had been to run away to Georgia and start a brand new life together. This was not Tim's ideal place to settle down, but it would have to do for now since his mother had a cabin there. It used to be his grandmother's, and he had always hated when he and his family vacationed there. Maybe it would be different with Sandy. Though she was too perky for his taste, she was pretty, and he thought that she might be trainable. If he could slap the spunk out of her, the relationship might work. Her constant giddiness annoyed him. Yanking his cigarette from his mouth was a stupid thing for her to do, and if she did it again, he'd have to smack some sense into her.

He had tried his best to put things into a smooth order of events. While Sandy was driving to Tennessee, he would be only a few hours behind her because he needed to drop the boys off at their fatal accident. After linking up with her, the two of them would continue driving to Georgia, leaving Robin to die in the trunk of her own car at a truck stop in Tennessee.

Tim looked at the time on his brother's cell phone. Quickly, he grabbed Robin's two blue suitcases from the bedroom. They were large and bulky, and he strained his back muscles placing them into the trunk of her car.

Now, the hard part was getting Robin to join her luggage without attracting attention. She would have to walk out to the car. There was no other way.

Tim untied her and removed the tape from her mouth. Then he used the gun to maneuver her through the apartment.

"I need to use the toilet," she cried.

"Fine, go." He stood by the bathroom door waiting for her to relieve herself. When she finished, he shoved her along.

"I need to wash my hands."

"No, you don't. Move. Hurry up." He carried a bag with him and a jacket over his arm to hide the gun that he had aimed on her.

"Please, don't kill us."

That's right, she had a baby in her womb. In all his spastic planning, he'd forgotten. "Move," he warned. "Keep walking. Your sister told me about the baby."

She cried hard. "Please. We can raise the baby together."

"You wanted Tony."

"But…"

He aimed the pistol at her belly. "Not another word."

When they reached Robin's car, he had her enter on the driver's side. Tim forced her to drive them to a closed, secluded car wash. Once inside a bay, he removed rope and tape from the bag, tied her limbs together, and taped her mouth closed. Carefully, he placed her into the trunk along side her suitcases.

He drove out of the car wash and back onto the main street. No one had seen a thing. The first part of his plan was successful. Tim took a big puff of his cigarette and exhaled, letting the tension ease.

As he pulled the car into the parking lot, Sandy was paying the taxi driver. He wiped the sweat from his forehead. All that lifting had strained his back muscles to the point where they were hurting. Tim sat in the car and watched the driver and Sandy unload box after box from the trunk and the car. They piled them all up on the curb. She had used that taxi as though it were a moving van. When the driver had removed the last two pieces of her luggage, two oversized pink suitcases, from his back seat, Tim stepped out of Robin's car.

Sandy ran to him. Immediately, she yanked the cigarette from his mouth and stomped on it. "Why do you keep doing that? You know you don't smoke," she said playfully.

His hand went back in a reaction and almost completed its forward motion to her face. No, he told himself, not yet. I'll handle this later.

She gave him a big hug and kiss. "I'm so happy to see you."

"Sandy," he held her down a bit trying to stop her bouncy motion, "we can celebrate when we're in Georgia at my mother's cabin." He gave her a map with the route highlighted. "Don't stop at a hotel. Drive straight through, and I'll meet you," he shuffled the smaller map on top of the larger one, "right here at this truck stop in Tennessee."

"We're not traveling together?"

"No. I have some things to do, so I'll meet you in Tennessee and then we'll drive together to Georgia."

"I don't understand."

"Let me handle things," he barked, agitated.

"Okay, Tony," she said quickly.

"When we meet in Tennessee…"

"Can't we meet sooner in Ohio or Indiana?"

"No."

"But I'll have to drive more than nine hours, and most of it in the dark. I'm not good driving tired."

"Just do it," he yelled.

"I'm sorry, Tony, I didn't mean to upset you. I'll meet you in Tennessee."

"That's my girl," he said with a quick smile. Once again, he was lost in lust over her pretty, little pout.

"I'm so happy to finally get to be with you forever!" She quickly hugged and kissed him.

He gently pushed her away. "Me, too, it's just that we have to take care of a few things first. I'm going through a divorce here."

"Is she keeping all of your stuff? When I left Bo, I took everything. He didn't try to stop me. As soon as I left his place, I had my things put in storage. I'm talking furniture, appliances, everything. I did that just before I checked into that hotel. I told you, remember?" She removed the small envelope with the key inside of it from her purse and held it out to him. The envelope had the storage unit's name and address on it. "Here, take the key to my unit. Take what you can out of the apartment, or you'll never get any of it back."

"I'll take care of it." He mindlessly shoved the envelope into his pant pocket.

"We'll get our furniture and things out of storage when we get our own place. That won't be too long, right?"

"Right," he agreed. Then the two of them loaded his brother's blue Avenger with her boxes.

"My suitcases aren't going to fit."

He walked quickly over to her two pieces of pink luggage and picked them up. "Owe." He grimaced in pain. "What do you have in here, the kitchen sink?"

"No, a dead body," she laughed.

Tim suddenly looked panicked, thinking that somehow his perfect plan could fail. "Yeah, right," he mustered a weak laugh.

"Oh, Tony, I'm so excited!"

He opened the back door on the driver's side of Robin's car and placed the suitcases inside. "There's no room in the trunk of this car either, so don't open it."

"I'm driving your wife's car? Why didn't she take it to Tennessee?"

"It's mine now. She didn't want it."

"Oh," Sandy commented slowly at the odd news. "She took a plane to her mom's?"

"No more questions," Tim said agitated.

"Okay. Um, can you put my suitcases in the trunk?"

"I just told you, this trunk is full. Don't open it!"

"That's right. You had to pack your stuff, too. I'm sorry."

He caught the fearful look in her eyes and realized that he had yelled harshly. "Sweetie, you'll never get it shut if you do," he said softly.

"What if I get tired? Wouldn't one overnight hotel stay be all right?"

"No, you can rest your eyes at a rest stop. Take a few catnaps, but no hotels."

"Tony, I didn't know you were so cheap. Well, I hope you're not going to turn down lovemaking." She smiled and gave him a long, slow kiss on the lips. Pulling gently away, Sandy whispered, "Let's go into the apartment."

His sexual desire vanished. "Sandy, there's no time. You have to leave right now. I'll meet you at that truck stop. Don't lose your maps. Call me if you have a problem. Remember, no hotels."

Sandy frowned. "Bye."

Tim looked at her pouting face and remembered that he needed her right now. "I'm sorry. I promise we'll make love in Georgia, as soon as we get to the cabin." After one last kiss, he waved goodbye to her. On his way into the building, he looked up and saw the curtains move on the front window in the apartment next to his. "Nosey broad, if only I had the time," he muttered.

CHAPTER 36

Laura

Laura let the curtain fall. It's none of my business what the neighbors do, she thought and continued to pet Kittykay. Then she pulled her cell phone from the clip on her pant waist and called her mother. "Mom, I'm here at my apartment. I'm just picking up some more clothes."

A half an hour later, she and her mother were still talking. "Mom, if I don't get off the phone with you, I'll never get there. I love you, too, bye." Laura removed the cat from her lap, picked up her bag of clothes, and grabbed her purse.

Jill entered carrying two bags of groceries. "I'm glad you're here."

"I was just about to leave."

"Stay for a few minutes. I want to tell you something." Jill set the grocery bags on the kitchen counter, rushed into the living room, and sat on the couch.

"Lilly Henkerson was here. She used the phone." Laura sat in the recliner.

"Again?"

"She thinks that you're nice."

"I am. I keep telling you that."

"Tony and Robin wouldn't answer the door when she knocked, and they wouldn't answer their phone when she called."

"I told you something is wrong over there. Why was she trying to reach them? Did she tell you?"

"She said that her son, Tim, is in the hospital, and he needs a kidney to live. Tony knows about it, but he hasn't returned to the hospital. I don't think he wants to donate a kidney. He and Robin were home that whole entire time that she was here. I know because right after she left, they left. Tony put two huge suitcases in Robin's car and drove away. Then Tony came back, and get this, his girlfriend stepped out of a taxi. She had a ton of boxes that they loaded into his car. He put two huge suitcases into Robin's car again, and his girlfriend drove away."

"In his wife's car?"

"Yes."

"Wow, I don't believe this."

"I saw it."

"That's what I don't believe. You were spying on them."

"Oh, no, I wasn't."

"You just told me…"

"Yeah, I was watching them, but not like you. I was watching them inadvertently. I just happened to be looking out the window while I was petting my cat."

"Sure. Okay, whatever you say. I, inadvertently, ran into Tony this morning when his girlfriend was leaving his apartment. Robin came home right after that. I wanted to tell her."

"You didn't, did you?"

"No."

Laura looked relieved. "Good, because it's not your business."

"Not then I didn't."

"What? Do you mean to tell me that you told her?"

"Yes. Don't worry. She knew already."

"Why would you even tell her?"

"I thought that if I told her that he was cheating on her, maybe she would come to her senses and leave him."

"Are you out of your mind?"

"He beats her, and I think that she should leave him."

"You don't even know her."

"Do you have to know someone in order to help them? Is there a handbook with rules?"

"Who did you help? Tony just sent his girlfriend off on a trip in his wife's car."

"I guess no one." She looked guilty. "You know, his girlfriend looks familiar."

"I thought so, too."

"Where have we seen her before?" Jill asked.

"I don't know."

A couple of seconds later, Jill called out, "I know where: your junk drawer." She ran over to the kitchen, opened the drawer, and pulled out the silver keychain with the plastic case and picture. She showed it to Laura.

"That's her."

"Don't get mad, but I did try to follow Tony and Robin earlier."

"What?"

"I thought he was going to hurt her. He was yanking her down the hallway, squeezing her arm, and pulling her. She even said that he was hurting her."

"What did you think that you were going to do?"

"I don't know, I just…I don't know. Anyway, I lost them in traffic, and I came back here."

"You are officially crazy."

"Why?"

"You were tailing the neighbors."

"Wait, there's more."

"You're kidding."

"I was sitting here by the window, and I, inadvertently, saw them come back with a small boy who was crying."

"You did not see them inadvertently. Just quit using the word. You were having a stakeout right here in my living room."

"No, I was just sitting where you are now, and I was petting your cat."

"I have never seen you pet my cat."

"Anyway, when I went over to their apartment, I asked about the boy, and Robin said that he was a relative. What was strange is that he was nowhere in sight."

"You went over there?"

"To borrow an egg."

"I have eggs."

"I didn't really want one. I just wanted to see if that boy was all right. I went over there twice, and I still didn't see him."

"You went there again?"

"To borrow another egg. And, I still didn't see the boy anywhere."

"Maybe he was in a bedroom."

"No, I checked."

"I'm not even going to ask how you managed to do that."

"It gets weirder. I went over there again to borrow some milk."

"You're kidding. They must think I don't have any food in this place."

"Tony yelled at me, and he wouldn't let me talk to Robin."

"What did he say?"

"No, we don't have any milk."

"So, that sounds normal enough. And, how can you blame him for raising his voice? You were bugging them."

"He wouldn't let me talk to Robin. He said that she was sleeping, and I had just talked to her moments earlier, so I know he was lying."

"She probably told him to lie for her. Don't you get it? You're a nuisance."

"No, I'm not. Listen, I saw Tony leave, so I knocked on their door again, and no one answered. I mean I pounded on that door. There is no way that they could have been sleeping."

"Good heavens! Why do you keep bothering them?"

"I think something's wrong over there."

"Well, it's not. Get that crazy notion out of your mind and leave those people alone."

"I tried. That's why I went to the store. I figured I'd shop and maybe buy some sugarless cookies."

"Since when do you eat sugarless cookies?"

"Robin said that the boy was diabetic."

"Oh, my god! You were planning to go over to their apartment again."

"I'm worried about the boy and Robin."

"The boy's a relative just like she said he was, and Robin's an adult who can make her own decisions. Leave it alone."

"What if Tony kidnapped that boy?"

"That's ridiculous. Why would he want to do that? You seriously need to find a hobby."

"Where did the boy go?"

"When he woke up from his nap, his parents probably came to get him. I'm sure he's safe and sound at home, and Robin is fine. I just told you that I saw her leave with Tony. She's okay."

"Unless he killed her."

"Jill, he put suitcases in the trunk. I saw him. He probably dropped her off at the airport. Good grief! Why can't you be like normal people and think about what would be more plausible? I believe Tony is having an affair, but I don't believe he's running around killing and kidnapping people. I've known him for a few years now, and he's always been friendly: always willing to help the neighbors. He helps the Greenways quite a bit. They're an elderly couple that live downstairs, and he is very good to them. So, when you say that he's an evil monster, it's hard to believe."

"You said that you didn't know him, and now you're saying you do."

"Well, I don't know, know him! What little things I do know about him speak for his character. That's all I'm saying."

"What about that little thing where he beats his wife?" Jill asked raising her voice in frustration. "What does that say about his character?"

"Okay, you've got me there, but I've never witnessed him beating her."

"You said they fight."

"No, I said they argue and yell. I've never heard them beating each other."

"I did."

"You think you did."

"What about her bruises? I saw them."

"She's clumsy."

Jill's cell phone buzzed and her ring tone began playing loud rap music. She looked at the caller ID and smiled, excited. "It's Danny."

"Good," Laura said sounding relieved.

"Sure. I'm at Laura's apartment. Do you remember how to get here? Oh, okay. What time? Sounds great. I'll see you in an hour. I love you, too. Bye." She ended the call and smiled at Laura. "Danny wants me to meet him up at the sport bar around the corner."

Laura smiled. "Thank goodness. Now, you can forget all this silliness and focus on something that is real, like your own life."

"Maybe you're right. My imagination could have gotten the best of me. After all, I wasn't watching their door the whole entire time."

"That's right. Now, worry about planning your wedding. Gee, look at the time. I have to get going; my mother will get worried."

"Does she worry this bad when you're not staying with her?"

"No. That's why I don't live with her." Laura smiled at her cat. "Oh, come here, baby. Momma wants to say good-bye to you."

"Your cat is spoiled, and it eats too much. I had to buy it some more food." Jill walked away and headed into the bathroom. "I have to go and get ready."

Laura walked into the kitchen and put Jill's two bags of groceries away. Then she picked up her bag of clothes and her purse and headed to the door. Kittykay meowed. Laura bent down, petted her, and whispered, "Oh, I miss you, too. I'll be back pretty soon. Grandma is getting better everyday. Now, you be good while I'm away."

As she opened the door, Kittykay shot into the hallway and ran to the Henkersons' apartment. Laura dropped her bag and purse and ran after her. "What are you doing? Kittykay, come here." She called out. "Get back here."

The cat meowed and pawed at the Henkersons' door. Laura reached down to grab her, but she was too late. Her cat slid into their apartment opening the door wider.

"Damn it." Laura grabbed the doorknob, pulled the door toward her, and knocked on it. No one answered. She sighed nervously and looked at her own opened apartment door and thought of soliciting Jill's help. After deciding not to, she opened the Henkersons' door farther. "Yoohoo! Anyone in here? It's me, Laura, from next door." She walked into their apartment.

"Hello. Hello." Laura walked through the living room and down the hallway where she saw her cat. She could hear the bathroom fan on, and she thought about knocking on the door to let whoever was in there know that she was in the apartment, but it seemed too awkward. She thought that it would be best just to grab her cat and get out quickly.

CHAPTER 37

Fred Greenway

Edna was feeling better. She walked into the living room and sat on the couch. "Fred," she called out to the kitchen.

He came running to her. "What is it, dear?"

"Where's our television?"

"Whoever broke into our place, took it."

"Did you call the police yet?"

"I wanted to get a good look around first to see if anything else was stolen. Do you see anything else missing?"

"No. How did they get in?"

"I don't know. The door looks fine, and the windows were all shut and locked."

"Do you think that Tony forgot to lock our door?"

"I tried to talk to him earlier, but he wasn't home. He's probably home now. I'll go try again. Do you want me to turn the radio on for you?"

"No. I wanted to watch my favorite cooking show."

Fred knew how much his wife suffered with pain, and now he was witnessing her being denied the smallest of pleasures. Upset, he said, "I'll find a way to get us another television." He fixed her a cup of tea before he left.

As Fred walked the hallway, he didn't feel safe anymore, not like he used to. Each step up the stairs brought him thoughts of suspicion about the newest tenant in the building, the newly hired maintenance man, and the shifty looking mail woman. Before he reached the Henkersons' apartment, he saw a bag and a purse on the floor in the hallway just in front of Laura's partially opened door. He picked them up and called inside the apartment, "Hello, Laura." Stepping in all the way, he walked into the kitchen. Fred set the purse inside the bag and placed it on one of the chairs next to the table. He proceeded back into the living room and headed down her hallway. There was music playing in the bathroom, and the shower was running. Afraid to scare her, he returned to the kitchen and looked around for something to write on. There was a pad of paper and an ink pen on the counter. He wrote a note: Laura, I found your purse and bag of clothes in the hallway near your door. After signing his name on it, Fred placed it on the table. As he left, he locked and closed the door.

CHAPTER 38

KittyKay

The black and white cat slipped into a back room at the end of the hall and crawled under the bed. Laura followed and saw its tail disappear under the bed's black skirt. "I'm going to kill you when I catch you," Laura whispered as she squatted and reached under the bed. Her grasp was too slow, and she missed. "Damn it," she whispered, dropping to her knees and pulling up the skirt. A quick glance under the bed, and she yanked the skirt back down. I did not just see that boy tied up under the bed, she told herself, frightened. Laura slowly lifted the skirt. This time her hands were shaking. Looking at Billy in disbelief, she heard the bathroom door open. Oh, my god she screamed inside her mind and dove under the bed next to him.

She listened to Tim walking down the hallway and into the bedroom. Laura saw his black boots and then the knee of his blue jeans as he knelt down. His hand reached out towards her as he groped under the bed. Laura backed away, shoving Billy over.

"Hello, Tony, it's me." Fred's voice called out.

Tim stood up fast. "I'll be right there," he hollered and hurried into the living room. "How did you get in?" he demanded.

"The door was open."

"I had it locked."

"Oh, look, you're right. The bottom lock is turned, but you must not have had it pulled shut. Maybe that's what happened when you left my apartment this morning."

"What do you want?" he snapped.

"You know when I asked you to lock the door this morning?"

"I did."

"Someone took our television, tore up the place, and took our money. Maybe, you didn't pull the door all the way shut when you left."

"I told you I shut it. I'm busy right now."

"There was no forced entry. Did you see anyone in the hallway when you left?"

"No."

"That television means a lot to Edna. She's sick you know and…" He began to cough.

Laura heard Fred say, "I hope you don't mind if I get some water from the kitchen. Hey, that's my television."

As she listened to their voices, she tried to untie the knots on the ropes binding Billy's hands and feet. Even the gag around his mouth had an incredibly tight knot. Hopelessly, she gave up. "I'm going to get help," she whispered to him and crawled out from under the bed just in time to see Kittykay jump on top of the dresser and begin playing with a glass, perfume bottle. Laura quietly walked over to her cat and gently picked her up. Her mind raced, searching for solutions. I can't yell for Fred to help, he'd get hurt or killed. I can't call the police, my phone will beep. It even beeps while I'm turning down the sound. I'll text. How do I send a text to the police? I'll send it to Jill. I've got to put my cat somewhere: the closet; I'll put her in there.

Carefully, she opened the closet door and nearly gasped when she saw the small boy that Jill had described. His pleading eyes looked up at her. "I'll save us," she whispered. Oh, God, get us out here safely, she prayed. Then unable to think straight, she opened the middle drawer on the dresser, pulled the clothes out, and she shoved them under the bed. Then she placed her cat inside the drawer and quietly pushed it shut. Laura then pulled out her cell phone and took a picture of the boy in the closet and of Billy under the bed. She sent the pictures to Jill's cell phone along with a text message that read: HELP US.

Desperately, Laura looked out the window, down at the grass and the sidewalk below, and at the tops of the trees. Frantically, she searched the room and saw the broken doorframe. Finally, her eyes caught sight of a metal flashlight on the floor. Picking it up, she felt its weight and held onto it tightly. Then Laura remembered the perfume bottle on the dresser had a spray nozzle. After arming herself with her weapons, she crept behind the bedroom door and waited.

Fred's voice was louder. "If you're in some kind of trouble, Tony, I might be able to…"

"I was going to fix it for you. That's all."

"There's nothing wrong with it."

"Take it and get out."

"Just give me my key, and you return my television. I'll call the police if you don't."

"Fine, old man."

"What are you doing? You can't just leave it in the hallway."

Laura heard the apartment door slam shut. She raised the flashlight and the perfume bottle into the air and took a deep breath. I can do this, she thought to herself. I can do this.

"Meow. Meow. Meow. Meow."

She heard the monster storm into the room and head straight for the dresser. Laura realized that as soon as he opened that drawer, he'd know someone was in the apartment, and he'd soon find her and kill her.

Tim opened the drawer, and out sprang Kittykay. She hissed at him, leaped through the air, and landed on the bed. The cat leaped off and ran out of the room. He chased after her.

Laura told herself to run after him and attack him from behind. Hitting him by surprise would be the only way that she could accomplish an escape, but she couldn't move. Fear made her legs freeze.

The cat was hissing and racing around the apartment, dodging Tim's grasping hands and stomping boots. Kittykay climbed the curtains, leaped onto the living room window ledge, and leaned on the screen.

"Gottcha," Tim said through clinched teeth, squeezing the cat's small, furry neck with his large hands.

"Meee Ow," the cat cried, struggling to free itself. It pulled its back paws up onto the top of Tim's hands and scratched him deep with its razor, sharp claws.

"Ahhh," he cried out and threw the cat into the screen.

Kittykay tumbled out of the window along with the screen. She landed on her paws and took off running to a nearby tree.

Tim cursed and stomped through the apartment. "Come out, Jill. I know you're in here. You'll pay for these scratches." Blood dripped down both of his hands and onto the carpet. He stormed into the kitchen, lifted the tablecloth, and looked under the table. Tim stomped back into the living room, looked behind the couch, and opened the living room closet door. After searching through the coats hanging up, he stormed into the bathroom and yanked the shower curtain onto the floor.

Laura listened to him as he raged through the apartment like a storm. She decided that she had better run for the door, but it was too late. His eyes were looking at her through the open cracks between the door's hinges.

Tim grabbed the doorknob and yanked the door so that Laura was exposed. "Who are you?" he demanded.

"I'm Laura. I just, I just, I my cat. I my, I was getting my cat tha.. that's all. I'm sorry, Tony. I should have knocked, but the door was open, and I just wanted to get my cat."

"So, hiding under the bed were you?"

She shook her head. "No."

"Hiding in the closet?"

"No." She knew that this was it. If she didn't run away now, it would be too late for her. She flung the flashlight up over her head and slammed it at his face while spraying the perfume into his eyes.

He knocked the perfume bottle to the floor, took hold of the flashlight, and grabbed a handful of her hair. Pulling her out from behind the door, Tim squeezed her neck.

"No!" she screamed, struggling to free herself. "Let me go!"

Those were her last words. Tim punched her once on the side of her head and everything turned black as she sank to the floor. He carried her limp body over to the bed and threw her down. He watched the side of her head bounce off the headboard and her cell phone bounce into the air. Immediately, he grabbed the small, digital device and shoved it into his pant pocket.

Within seconds, Laura became conscious again and tried to pull herself into a sitting position. She felt the side of her head.

Tim pulled out the pistol and pointed it at her. "Wipe the blood off your face."

She felt her warm blood dripping down the side of her face. Laura tried wiping it off with her hands. I'm hurt, she thought, looking at her red covered hands.

"Use the sheet."

She wiped her hands on the sheet, and then pulled the sheet up to the side of her head and wiped it. Laura wadded up a corner of the sheet and held it firmly to her head.

"Get over here."

She dropped the sheet and followed his orders. Frightened and shaky, she stood next to him.

"Open the closet. Pull him out."

Laura did it and waited further instruction. She watched him move the aim of the pistol from herself to the young boy.

Tim pulled the bedspread up. "Drag him out."

Laura crawled partially under the bed. Billy was heavy, and it was difficult for her to get him.

"Hurry up!" Tim shouted and kicked her.

She pulled and pulled again until Billy was out from under the bed. Laura stood up, exhausted.

"Untie the boys."

Laura easily untied Jeff, but Billy's ropes had tighter knots. It took longer, and Tim continued to kick and hit her throughout the ordeal.

"I said hurry." He kicked her in the back.

Laura jumped from the pain. "I'm trying," she cried and resumed working on the knot behind Billy's back. Finally, she removed it.

"Remove the gag in his mouth."

Laura tried, but she was unsuccessful. Tim had to do it, and he was rough about it, cutting Billy's lips.

Jeff's mouth had tape across it. He removed it himself, hurting his own lips. While he had already been crying, he was now crying even more.

Tim placed a jacket over his arm and continued to aim the gun on Jeff. Then he slowly walked Laura, Billy, and Jeff to the front door. "Stop!" He examined them, opened the living room closet door, and removed Tony's blue hooded sweatshirt: the only piece of clothing with a hood. Shoving it at Laura, he ordered, "Put it on."

She quickly did as he ordered. Her hands were shaking.

"Pull the hood up."

Again, she obeyed his demand. Laura could feel hot tears sliding down her cheeks.

"All of you quit crying. Now!"

Jeff wiped his eyes. "I'm trying to stop," he sniffled.

"Try harder. Walk. All of you. Come on. Walk," he ordered. Then, he guided them out of the apartment, out of the building, and next to his brother's blue Avenger. Tim looked up at Laura's apartment window, but he didn't see Jill. In fact, the curtains were drawn. He scanned the parking lot and didn't see anyone. Keeping Jeff next to him, he looked at Laura and Billy. "You two, unload these boxes. Throw them all in the dumpster."

They did as he ordered. Soon, all of Sandy's boxes were out of the car and there was room for everyone.

Tim had Laura drive the car into the same desolate car wash as he had made his sister-in-law drive to earlier. He, then, tied and taped his victims. Both boys he shoved down into the back floorboards and put a blanket over each one. Laura, he tied, taped, and placed into the trunk.

CHAPTER 39

The Investigation

At 9:00 p.m., while Officers Hall and Dobbs were on the road, Detective Nettle called. Speaking to Hall, he said, "I didn't talk to Becky Norton, the owner of the Escort. Their next-door neighbor said they left on a camping trip."

"Her father didn't want me talking to her. I'm sure he's just trying to avoid us," Hall replied.

"Right now, I'm following a lead from a call in on the AMBER Alert. A dispatcher at the Taxis R4U thinks that Billy's picture on the television looks like the kid that was in his place tonight," Nettle said.

"We already questioned the dispatchers there, and not one of them said that they had seen Billy," Hall explained.

"This guy said that you were there, but now he thinks that the kid gave him a fake name."

"We showed him a picture."

"Right, well, the guy came forward and admitted that a kid fitting Billy's description came in tonight. He didn't want to say anything because he broke the company's policy and let the boy use a taxi. He said that the kid told him he needed to see his dying grandmother, and he felt sorry for him, but not enough to give him a deal. He charged the boy fifty dollars. He also let the boy keep his bicycle in a back room. Did Billy have a blue mountain bike?"

Mark Hall examined his notepad that he carried in his front pocket. "Yes, he did," he answered.

"What is it?" John asked anxiously.

"The driver said that the boy's fifty dollar bill had honor roll written on it," Nettle added.

"I don't know about that. I'll check." Mark turned to John. "Did Billy have a fifty with the words honor roll on it?"

"Yes, yes he did! Did they find him?"

"Not yet, John." Mark turned his attention to the phone. "Nettle, that was Billy's fifty."

"I thought so. I'm heading to the apartment complex where Billy was dropped off," Nettle reported.

"Send me the address."

"Let me check it out first before you get John in on this."

"What is it? Tell me!" John demanded.

"Too late, Nettle. Give me the address," Mark said.

"I'm sending it to you now. See it on your screen yet?"

Hall glanced at his computer screen. "Got it."

"Hall, talk to me. Is this where the boys are at?" John yelled.

"John, it's just a lead. No one is sure of anything yet," Mark explained.

He didn't care. John studied the address on the screen, hit the siren and flashing lights, and sped to the destination.

Detective Nettle and three police officers arrived at the apartment building where Billy Dobb's taxi had taken him. "Officers Dobbs and Hall are on their way over," Nettle warned his team. "Keep an eye on Dobbs."

Charles Digger was alarmed at the sudden intrusion. "Is there a problem?"

"Are you the manager?" Nettle asked.

"Yes. I'm Charles Digger."

"We're investigating a case of missing children. Have you seen either one of these boys?" Nettle held out a picture to him.

"No."

"Mr. Digger, generate a list for me with all your tenants names," Nettle ordered.

Then, he looked at his team. "Two of you start door to door searches. One of you, stay here and assist me."

Two officers left immediately. They each had a picture of the boys.

Nettle waited patiently while Charles Digger went through his computer's database and created the tenant list. Once it was ready, Detective Nettle ordered the manager to step aside while he examined it. He was staring hard at the monitor screen, scrutinizing each name, when Officer Dobbs and Officer Hall arrived. Soon, the officers were reading over his shoulders. Hall saw the name first. "Henkerson," he shouted out. "That was the name of the victim we found."

John and Mark quickly memorized the building and apartment number. They bolted out of the manager's office.

"Hold on. We can't be sure that it's that apartment," Nettle warned. He and the other officer ran in pursuit after them.

Charles Digger opened his desk drawer and grabbed the duplicate key for the Henkersons' apartment. "Wait, I have a key," he hollered, chasing after them.

Officer Dobbs saw a male tenant exiting the building, so he picked up speed and rushed the door before it closed, nearly knocking the man down. Dobbs ran to the Henkersons' apartment and kicked the door open. A frantic look around, told him that he had the right place. Someone had disheveled clothes from drawers and closets, had knocked the living room window screen out, and had broken the doorframe to the bedroom. There was blood on the carpet in the living room and on the bed sheets. "Billy! Jeff!" he called out almost in tears. He found Billy's orange backpack under the bed. Grabbing it and clutching it in his hands, he yelled for his oldest son. Then, he reached inside of it and found Billy's white baseball shirt. Crying, John let go of the backpack and held his son's game shirt up to his face.

The other officers along with his partner and the detective caught up to him and entered the apartment. The manager saw the broken door and immediately began to yell, "What did you do that for? I have the key in my hand. If you would have just waited a few seconds. What's a few seconds?"

John pulled the shirt away from his face, but continued to clutch it in his hands. "My sons' lives."

Mark put an arm around him. "John, I'm going to take you home to your wife."

The detective nodded in agreement. Then, he phoned his investigation team to meet him at the apartment. Right away, he put an APB out on the Henkersons' vehicles.

"I'm not going home without my sons," John shouted.

Mark backed off. "Okay. All right, John." He looked to Nettle for help.

"Hall and Dobbs, start questioning the neighbors," Nettle ordered. "My team will take care of the work in here."

John didn't move. Mark slowly pulled Billy's baseball shirt from his partner's hands. He then handed it to Nettle. "Come on, John. Let's go. Someone had to have heard or seen something."

Unaware that he was even walking, Dobbs let Hall lead him away from the apartment. Numb to his own anguish, he proceeded on as though he were in a nightmare that he knew had to eventually end.

CHAPTER 40

Jill

Jill thought she heard police sirens outside. She ran to the window and almost pulled the curtain back, but then she stopped herself. "No, I'm going to mind my own business." A short time later, she heard heavy footsteps running in the hallway. Quickly, she opened the apartment door.

One police officer kicked the Henkersons' door open. More officers entered the apartment with their guns drawn. Jill heard her cell phone and answered it. "Hi, Danny. I can't talk right now. The police are breaking into the neighbors' apartment. Let me call you back. Bye."

When the commotion had ended, Jill stepped into the hallway. "What's going on?" Jill asked the officers who were exiting the Henkersons' apartment.

Mark Hall's face was full of disappointment and worry. "We're looking for Tony and Robin Henkerson. Do you know where they are?"

"No."

"We're also looking for these two children." He showed her a picture of John's sons. "Have you seen them?"

"This one," she said pointing to Jeff's image.

"Where?" Dobbs asked anxiously.

"Here in the building. He was with Tony and Robin Henkerson."

"When?"

"Today, a little before six o'clock. What's going on?"

"Did you see them leave?"

"No. Robin said that boy was her relative."

"He's not. They kidnapped him."

"Oh, no!"

"If you hear or see anything, call us," was the last thing the officer said before he left.

Jill stood frozen in the hallway. It was true. She had been right. Calling Laura and saying so was the first thing she planned to do. On her way back into the apartment, she realized that while she had been out in the hallway, she had left the door open. Fearing the worst, she began calling for the cat, "Kittykay, where are you? Kittykay! Kittykay! Where are you? It's dinner time." She searched each room. "Kittykay. Kittykay." She opened the apartment door and looked down each end of the hallway. She walked quickly to the stairs and ran down them. She checked the laundry room and the mailroom. Jill saw the two officers again. They were entering someone's apartment. Jill could hear the tenant talking to them. She walked back up the stairs. This time, she stopped in front of the Henkersons' apartment. The door was hanging from the broken frame and there were detectives inside. Jill looked in and was shocked to see that the window was wide open without a screen. There was blood on the carpet in the living room. Now, she thought for sure that something bad had happened to Robin and those two missing boys.

One of the officers on the crime team spotted her. "Who are you?"

"The Henkersons' neighbor. Did you see a cat? I lost my friend's cat," she said almost apologetically. She knew that a missing cat was nothing compared to missing children.

"No."

Jill headed back into Laura's apartment and thought about shaking the cat's treat bag up and down the hallway. As she entered the kitchen, she noticed the piece of paper on the table. She read Fred Greenway's note, carefully. Jill glanced partially under the table and saw the bag with Laura's clothes and purse in it.

Quickly, she rushed to the living room window and opened the curtains. Under the lamplights, Jill saw Laura's car in the parking lot. Something was terribly wrong. Jill tried to call her on her cell phone, but there was no answer. This is when she noticed the text message. She picked up the message and opened the pictures. "No, no, no, no!"

Jill rushed back down the hallway to the detectives in the Henkersons' apartment and held out her cell phone. "Look! Look!"

"Lady, you can't come in here." The officer who had talked to her earlier, grabbed her.

"Look!"

After a quick glance and a closer look, he called out, "Detective Nettle, come look at this."

The detective rushed out of the bedroom and into the living room. "At what?"

The detective took hold of Jill's cell phone and viewed the pictures. Right away, he recognized Dobb's sons. He eyed Jill. "Who took these? Did you take these?"

"No. Laura sent them to me. She's missing. I thought she went to her mother's, but she didn't. Her car is still in the parking lot, and her purse and keys are in the apartment."

"Who's Laura?"

"Laura Knight. She's my best friend, and she lives in the apartment next door."

"Calm down. When did she leave the apartment?" Nettle asked.

"I don't know. I guess it was an hour ago, maybe two."

"All right, calm down." He glanced at one of the officers. "Take a report from her."

Hall and Dobbs returned to the Henkersons' apartment in time to witness Jill's report. When she spoke about the pictures on her cell phone, both officers looked at Nettle.

"Where's the pictures?" John asked upset. "Let me see them."

Detective Nettle shook his head. "John, it'll just upset you."

"Where's her cell phone?" John demanded.

"Okay, here." The detective regrettably handed the cell phone to him.

After John saw the alarming pictures, he was silent. Slowly, he handed the cell phone to his partner.

Mark was speechless. These were not only his long time partner's sons; they were his godsons.

Detective Nettle nodded to the officer taking Jill's report. "Continue."

The officer asked, "Why would Tony Henkerson want to take your friend? How's she involved?"

"I don't know." She shook her head, puzzled.

The detective could see that John was about to lose his self-control. Somehow, he had to get him to leave the building. Thinking fast, he said, "John, you and Mark drive to the hospital and question Tony Henkerson's mother. She's there with her other son, Tim. I'm certain now that Tony Henkerson tried to kill his brother. Hall, I'm going to send these pictures to your cell phone. Show them to her, and find out where he's at."

Nettle waited for John and Mark to leave the apartment. When he was certain that they would not hear him, he turned to three officers. "Go to the hospital and talk with the mother. Get information back to me as soon as you get something. Keep an eye on John."

CHAPTER 41

The News

Officer Mark Hall parked the patrol car into the parking lot near the main entrance. He hurried out of the vehicle and waited for his partner. "John, come on."

The frustration and fear showed on John Dobb's face as his anger and helplessness overtook him. "I'm a cop for Christ's sake."

"We'll find them. I promise," Mark reassured him.

John sat stunned. These were the same words said to every parent with a missing child. He knew that time was crucial: if children weren't found within so many hours, they were usually gone forever. Officer Dobbs now knew why Billy had stolen his pistol: he had gone to save his brother. If only he had come to him for help. Tears welled up in his eyes, and he felt too emotionally crippled to move.

"Come on, let's go."

He heard his partner's voice as though it were traveling from a long distance. His body ran on autopilot to move his legs, making them walk him into the hospital. It was as though he were having an out-of-body experience. His mind was lost in deep emotional torment, but his body kept moving mechanically on with the investigation.

Before the two of them made it past the information desk, three police officers burst through the main entrance doors. Hall and Dobbs looked a bit surprised.

"He sent us after you left," one of them explained.

Hall shrugged his shoulders. "Why? We've got this."

The officer shrugged his shoulders in return. "I don't know."

All five officers were now heading down the long hallway toward the intensive care unit. John was in the lead and the first to see the woman who he assumed to be Lilly Henkerson standing in the hallway. There she is, he thought, the mother of that, that, that...

Mark saw anger building up on John's face and that his hands were now clenched fists. "Hey, you stay right here."

He kept moving. All he saw was his target. It was quiet where he was at.

"Hey, I said stay here!" Mark shouted into his face.

John heard him this time. "No," he hollered back and took off running.

Mark and the other three officers chased after him. They had to stop him before he hurt her.

Lilly Henkerson, who had been looking down the hallway in the other direction, heard the yelling and turned to see the five officers rushing down the hallway toward her. She was frightened. Lilly no longer worried about flagging down a nurse to change her son's I.V. bag.

"What's going on?" she cried.

Hall reached out and grabbed Dobbs in a bear hug. "Stop!"

"I'm fine," he said. "I promise. I'm fine." He spoke his words as though he were coming out of a hypnotized trance.

Officers' questions flew at Lilly so fast; she didn't know which question to answer first. "I don't know where he is. What he's capable of...I don't know. What do you mean? No, he'd never harm anyone," she replied. Then, after seeing the pictures held out to her on Officer Hall's cell phone, she asked fearfully, "What is this?"

"Where is Tony?" Officer Mark Hall questioned.

Suddenly, she knew who they were looking for. "Tony's here. He's in that hospital bed. You're looking for my other son, Tim. He's capable of this." Now, she knew what had happened.

Nurse Sharon Thompson came from a nearby room carrying a full I.V. bag. She stopped to usher the people from the hallway. "You can't be here. Lilly, what is all this? Officers, what is this about? Go to the visitors' room."

No one listened to her. The officers left without answering her questions, and Lilly Henkerson remained in the hallway crying. "Give me a second," Sharon said. Then, she quickly walked into the patient's room and replaced the I.V. bag. After she finished, she walked Lilly Henkerson to the visitation room. "Please, sit down and tell me why the police were here. Did they find out who tried to kill your son?"

Lilly slowly sat in a chair. "Yes," she nodded her head sadly. "My other son."

"What?"

"Yes," she cried.

Disbelieving, Sharon asked, "Tony?"

"Tim. Tony's the one here in the hospital," she said through tears.

"Wow. So, my patient is Tony?"

"Tony's sure to die now. Tim will never give him a kidney."

Sharon's facial expression went from sorrow to fear. "My sister! Tim is with her. She was bruised. She said she fell. He must have hit her. She's pregnant. I have to save her."

"She's pregnant?" A glimpse of happiness showed in Lilly's eyes and then vanished. The fear for her daughter-in-law's and her grandchild's lives drowned it out.

CHAPTER 42

Robin's Plight

The situation was grave. The all-point bulletin on the Henkersons' vehicles did not develop any leads. There were officers searching the surrounding area. The news stations were broadcasting pictures of the missing boys and of Tim Henkerson's mug shot on an AMBER Alert. Radio announcers pleaded for citizens to help, requesting listeners to phone the police with any information about the suspects and the missing boys.

Sandy did not hear one word about Tim, the dangerous ex-con, armed with a weapon. She was busy listening to music on her CD player. It was blaring from the car speakers.

Robin heard it, too, and had been listening to it for hours while being smashed up against her luggage that was pressing painfully into her back. The weight of her baby on her abdomen, hurt.

She knew her and her baby's fate: Tim would stage a car accident. Who would know to save them? The answer was as depressing as it was obvious: no one. I'm sorry, baby. I'm so sorry, she thought repeatedly. I won't give up. I'll protect you.

Robin struggled to maneuver herself around. It was not easy to wiggle and flip herself over onto her stomach, but she did it after many exhausting attempts. Now, her hands that were tied behind her back could maybe grasp the latch. Several tries to stretch her fingers into the air and locate the latch were unsuccessful. She maneuvered some more, but she couldn't get her body high enough to make her hands form the connection to the plastic piece above her. Diligently working, she moved herself just enough to get her bound together feet in an effective position to kick the back of the seats.

Performing crunches and straightening her body were the only movements that brought her feet into contact with the back seats, but the impact was not strong enough to break the mechanism. The button to allow the seats to fall forward was only operable from inside the car. Perhaps, if I save my energy, she thought, maybe I can kick the seats so Sandy can hear me. I'll just have to wait until she turns the music down. The baby kicked her hard. Don't worry. I'll save us. We won't die in here. I promise. The heat was already getting to her, and with no water, she knew that she would dehydrate. How long will I be able to last? She wondered as the music blared. Surely, the car will need gas soon, and then maybe, somehow…

CHAPTER 43

Information

At eleven p.m., Officers Hall and Dobbs returned to Laura's apartment to gather more information about her. They updated Jill, letting her know that Tony was in the hospital and that his twin brother, Tim, had stolen his identity. They reviewed Jill's report seeing that Tim had a girlfriend. "You don't know the girlfriend's name?" Hall asked.

"No. I just know that she's driving Robin's car."

They thanked her and left. Moments later, after Jill had shut the door, she remembered the keychain. She didn't see it on the couch where she and Laura had left it. After searching, Jill found it between the cushions. Quickly, she ran down to the parking lot. "Officer!"

Officer Hall put the car window down. "Yes."

"Laura found this on the stairs yesterday. It's the picture of Tim's girlfriend."

"We'll be able to use this. Thanks."

As the police car was pulling away, the headlights lit up a huge oak tree next to the building and two eyes glowed. "Kittykay," Jill yelled out. "Hold on, I'm coming."

Now, she stood under the tree looking way up at the cat's dark shadow. "Kitty, Kittykay, come down."

"Meow, meow, meow, meow," the cat continued for some time.

"Get down here."

The cat made one long sound, "Meeooow."

Fred Greenway happened to look out of his window and saw Jill. He came outside. "What is going on?"

"Who are you?"

"I'm Fred Greenway."

Jill remembered that the note on the table had been signed by him. "I'm Jill. I'm apartment sitting for Laura Knight. I'm taking care of her cat." She looked up into the tree, and Kittykay meowed loudly.

Fred looked up at the noise and saw the dark silhouette of a cat on a limb, high up in the tree. Sounding sad, he said, "The police questioned me about when I saw her last and about that boy, Billy. I didn't even know that Tony had a twin."

"A lot of people didn't."

"Edna and I are praying for them all. Tony has always been so good to us. I should have known it wasn't him. He'd never steal from us."

"He had all of us fooled." Tears slid down her cheeks, and her voice became uneven as she uttered the words, "I have to… do… something." She sniffled, "But I…just…don't know…what."

There was a moment of silence, and then the cat meowed. "I'll get you a flashlight," Fred offered.

Jill didn't understand him at first. "Oh, you mean for the cat." She wiped her eyes and looked up the tree again. "Thanks."

It didn't take Fred long to bring her the flashlight. Soon, he was shining it at the tree while Jill climbed up. "Be careful. That's awfully high up. Maybe you should just wait for her to come down on her own. It would be awful if you fell. How will you carry her down once you get to her?"

Jill tried to tune him out. Not one word had been encouraging. The last thing she needed to hear were the thoughts that she was already thinking.

While she steadily, but slowly advanced toward the cat, Fred heard his wife yelling for him. "I'll be right back," he called up the tree and walked away with the light.

Jill balanced herself on two branches under her feet and held on tightly to two limbs above her head. Now, in the dark, she waited for Fred to return.

The minutes rolled by like hours. She began to panic. Perhaps he forgot about me. Now, what am I going to do? I can't even see to get down, she thought. When she was about to cry out for help, there came a light: two headlights from the car that just pulled into the parking lot. Seconds later, the driver turned on the brights. Now, the area was lit up well enough that once again, Jill could see Kittykay. Not knowing how much time that she had left before the driver turned off the headlights, she quickly climbed higher and scooted closer to the cat. Just as she was about to reach for her, Jill heard Danny's voice.

"What are you doing in that tree?"

"Oh," she said feeling relieved. It was comforting to know that he cared about her enough to come looking for her when she had not shown up at the bar. "I'm saving Laura's cat. Danny, she's missing," she cried.

"No, she's right there."

"Not the cat, I'm talking about Laura."

"What?"

"Yeah, that crazy neighbor took her."

"Come down. Let me get the cat."

"No, I'll get her." Jill climbed up the tree farther, and grabbed the cat. Now, she realized that she could not climb down and hold the cat.

"Just drop her. She's a cat. She'll land on her paws."

"No."

Danny climbed up the tree and stopped a branch lower than Jill. "Hand the cat to me."

Jill did so, and then climbed down just below Danny. "Okay, hand her back to me."

They did this until they were all safely out of the tree. By the time that Fred came back outside with the flashlight, Jill no longer needed it. She introduced him to her fiancé.

Danny turned off his brights, and he followed Jill into Laura's apartment. While she was telling what she knew about the Henkersons, the land phone rang. The caller ID read Anne Knight.

"Hello."

"Jill?"

"Yes."

"This is Laura's mother."

"I'm so sorry. I should have called you."

"The police were here. After they left, my cell phone rang. This is going to sound strange, but I can hear Laura's voice on it."

"What?"

"On my cell phone."

"What do you mean?"

"My phone rang, and I answered it, but no one said anything, but I can hear people in the background talking. Laura's name is on the caller I.D."

"Did you call the police?"

"Yes, but they haven't arrived yet."

"Is your hip well enough to drive? Could you drive that cell phone to the police station?"

"Oh, I would try, but my cell phone wasn't charged long enough, and I have it plugged into the wall. If I pull it out now, I think I'll lose my connection. I don't want to hang up on Laura. I'm scared. Could you…"

"I'll be right there," she promised before ending the call.

"What's going on?" Danny asked.

"I'll explain when I get back." She ran next door to the Henkersons' apartment. Now, there was only one officer left. Jill informed him about Anne Knight's cell phone and the possibility of a connection to the missing victims.

CHAPTER 44

Do What I Say

At 11:00 p.m., the car stopped. The music stopped, too. Robin rolled onto her back and kicked as much as she could against the top of the trunk. The rope around her legs limited movement so that she could barely get her feet to stretch up high enough to touch the metal. The impact was not what she had hoped it would be. The movement of lifting her legs with a baby in her womb was strenuous to the point of pain in her back. Her legs had finally stopped throbbing from the tightened rope. Now, they were just numb. She heard Sandy placing the nozzle into the tank. Again, she mustered her strength and kicked her bound legs. Finally, there was a rather loud thud sound. She'd loosened the ropes a bit with her movement. The reach with her feet was greater now. Robin kicked five times.

Sandy hurried into the driver's seat. Quickly, she drove the car around to the back of the gas station. Safe now behind a brick wall, she yelled at the trunk. "Who are you?"

The muffled sound came back. "Mmmmm. Mmmmm. Mmmmmm."

Sandy couldn't believe it. This is exactly what she had feared when she heard the noise. Someone was actually in the trunk.

"Mmmmm. Mmmmm. Mmmmmm."

Sandy pulled her cell phone out of her purse and phoned Tony's cell phone.

"What?" Tim demanded, sounding irritated.

Glancing around to make sure no one would hear her, she whispered gratingly, "Who's in the trunk?"

"It's Robin. Don't let her out."

"Your wife?"

"Don't let her out."

"Why is she in there? What are you thinking of doing? I don't understand…"

"Sandy, shut up. Listen to me. Robin found out about us leaving, and she said that she was going to kill you."

"You said she was giving you a divorce. You said she gave you her car. You…"

"Listen to me."

"What are you doing? Why…"

"Stop talking. Listen to me. It's for your own safety that she's in the trunk. Don't let her out." There was a loud horn honk. Then, Tim yelled out, "Asshole!"

"What?"

"Not you," he said sounding agitated. "Someone tried to cut me off."

"Where are you? Are you near me? What are we going to do?"

"I'll be with you soon. Don't let Robin out of the trunk. Follow the plan. I'll meet you in Tennessee."

"We can't just leave her in the trunk. She'll die."

"No, she won't. What she'll do is calm down."

"When are we letting her out?"

"We aren't. We'll leave her in Tennessee, and then when we are on our way to Georgia, I'll call someone to let her out. Are you driving right now?"

"No."

"I told you not to stop."

"I needed gas. This is kidnapping. We'll get in trouble. The police will come after us."

"She threatened you. It's self defense."

"Are you sure?"

"Look, I don't have time for this right now. I'm in the middle of something. Just do what I say. Stay with the plan, and don't let her out of the trunk unless you want her to kill you."

"Tony, this just doesn't…"

"You love me right?"

"Yes."

"Then, trust me, and don't stop again. You're going to mess everything up. Stick to the plan."

"Tony. Tony? Tony?" She put her cell phone back into her purse and looked hard at the trunk. Sandy thought about opening it, just to make sure that Robin was okay, but then she thought about Bo. He had tried to kill Tony with his bare hands the night he had found out about the affair. Robin could be same way. And, after all, it's not like Tony had a plan to kill her or anything. He was not that kind of person. He was just diffusing a violent situation. In all the time that she'd known him, he had always been gentle and kind. Lately, there had been some changes, but he was under pressure with making the final decision to be with her. Apprehensively, she climbed back into the driver's seat and started the car. Once more, she heard the thump noise. Slowly, she turned the CD player on and the volume up.

CHAPTER 45

Connection

At Mrs. Knight's house, Anne, Jill and Danny, along with three detectives and five police officers, heard the conversation between Tim Henkerson and Sandy. Though muffled, they were able to make out the information that Sandy was traveling to Tennessee. Quickly, the detectives mapped out routes from Michigan and radioed the officers in the police helicopters.

The detectives had connected Anne Knight's cell phone to a speaker that increased the volume ten times the phone's normal capacity. Everyone sat quietly, straining to listen to any sound coming through Laura's cell phone.

The lead detective and Officer John Dobbs stepped outside. They walked over to the patio in the backyard.

"It's luck that he accidentally made that phone call. It's happened to me before. I was at dinner with my wife, and I had my cell phone in the carrier you know. I hit a button by accident, and my sister heard me talking with my wife at dinner. Now, most phones have locks."

Officer John Dobbs frowned. "Have you found anything else?"

"Not really. The ditch wasn't the crime scene. It was just where Tony Henkerson's body was dumped. A neighbor said that she heard fighting in Tony's apartment on Friday night. That's probably when it happened. The bag was taken from an ambulance that Tim robbed about a week ago. During our search at his mother's house, we found a stethoscope, and a couple other medical supplies reported missing from that ambulance." He took a moment to think about things. "Oh, we found a few small items inside the bag. They probably fell out of Tony's pocket. They were nothing of importance: a nickel, a pack of gum, small stuff like that."

"I want to know exactly what they were."

The lead detective pulled his notepad from his pocket. He read off the items, "a piece of gum, a nickel, and a key. Nothing important."

"What about the gas can?"

"It was from a gas station that had been robbed early, Saturday morning. The price tag was still on it."

"This guy is so sloppy. Why haven't we caught him yet?" Dobbs asked frustrated.

"We will."

Officer Mark Hall exited the house and ran over to them. "Hurry, come back inside."

The atmosphere of the room was tense. Everyone quietly listened. They heard sounds of car doors shutting and Tim's voice yelling out, "Move." Then, there was a lot of breathing, what sounded like someone yelling in pain, and possibly Tim struggling with someone. Billy's voice yelled out, "Stop or I'll shoot." This surprised everyone. One shot sounded, and then Tim screamed out in pain.

Hope rose in the listeners. Billy had shot Tim Henkerson. Then Billy's voice was heard again. This time he was crying out in pain. Two more shots sounded and then a fourth shot. There were sounds of yelling and screaming in the background. Abruptly, the call ended.

It was quiet in the room. No one knew what to say. John spoke first. "Where are they?" he cried.

"Go home to your wife. Officer Hall, take him home," Detective Nettle commanded.

"No," John said, shaking his head. "No, I'm not going home until they're found."

Anne Knight hugged Jill, "My poor Laura," she cried.

"They'll find her," Jill said, wiping her own tears away. "They'll find all three of them."

At midnight, the detectives and the police left. Only Jill and Danny remained at Anne Knight's house. The three of them were miserably disappointed.

"Anne, come with us to Laura's apartment. There's no reason to sit and wait alone," Jill said.

"Thank you," Anne accepted graciously.

They were quiet on the ride to the apartment. As they walked into the building, there was a solemn silence. Anne walked slowly to the Henkersons' empty apartment. The entrance was closed off with crime tape. She peered inside.

"Anne, come on. I'll make us something to eat," Jill said as she touched her shoulder and guided her next door.

Danny offered to cook. He searched the cabinets and the refrigerator. "How does ham and cheese omelets sound?"

"Good. Make some coffee, too," Jill called back from the living room.

As soon as he opened the first egg carton, he saw the message: HELP! HE IS GOING TO KILL THE BOY IN BASEMENT IN WOODS NEAR PARK. "Jill, come here."

"I'm getting a pillow for Anne. Hold on."

"No! Now! Get in here."

She hurried into the kitchen. "What is it?"

"Look," he said, holding the egg carton out to her.

"Call the police, Danny."

After he reported the message to Detective Nettle, he looked at Jill. "Honey, it's not your fault."

"It is, too. I should have known she was trying to tell me something. I'm so stupid."

Danny held her. "No, sweetheart. It's not your fault. Don't blame yourself."

Anne ran into the kitchen. When she learned what the commotion was about, she cried along with Jill. Hope and fear stirred in the air.

Fifteen minutes later, a female detective arrived to take the egg carton as evidence. She assured everyone that Detective Nettle received the message, and his team was already searching all wooded areas near the parks.

CHAPTER 46

Bo's Call

While driving, Sandy reached her hand into her purse to feel around for a pack of gum. That was when she felt her phone vibrate. She pulled it out of her purse and turned the music down. "Tony?" she answered.

"No, it's me, Bo."

"Oh. Quit calling me."

"Don't hang up. The police are looking for you."

"What?"

"I saw a picture of you on the news. It looks like you anyway. They said that you were driving Robin Henkerson's car. Are you?"

"What?" she screamed.

"They don't know your name. They're calling you the mystery woman."

"What else did they say?" she demanded as she pulled the car off the highway and onto a side street.

"They said that Tony's twin brother stole his identity. That's who you're with."

"What?" she asked in disbelief.

"And, they said that he kidnapped two little boys, a police officer's children. Are you helping him?"

"No!" she shouted alarmed. "No!" Suddenly, Tony's smoking, his short temper, and his mood changes made sense. Sandy drove into a parking lot of a closed store. She shut off the engine. "What about Tony? Where is he?"

"I don't know, but, Sandy, I'll take you back. I mean, if you didn't have anything to do with this. Well, even if you did, I'll take you back."

Sandy ended the call and phoned 911. Then after giving the police her location, she pushed the trunk release button on her keypad. The trunk popped open. Apprehensively, Sandy looked inside to see Robin scrunched up against her luggage inside the small space with her limbs bound by rope and her mouth taped shut. Her skin was an unnatural, pasty white. Shocked by the image, Sandy wanted to scream. She had not imagined that Robin would be dead. Pacing back and forth near the trunk, she yelled, "Oh no! She's dead! She's dead!" Then, she lowered her voice and asked, "What am I going to do?"

Just then, Robin's left foot twitched. Sandy cried out, "Thank God, you're alive. I'm sorry. I didn't know. He said that you wanted to kill me, that you were dangerous. I'm sorry. He lied to me." She removed the tape from Robin's mouth.

"Water."

Sandy ran to the front of the car and pulled her Coke container from the center holder. She ran back to Robin. "Drink this." Sandy pulled Robin up into a sitting position and held the straw toward her mouth.

Robin sipped until she drained the cup. Then, Sandy untied her arms, hands, legs, and feet. "Let me help you get out."

"No. My legs and feet are too numb."

"I'm so sorry." Sandy helped Robin rub her numb feet.

"I don't blame you."

"I'm sorry about cheating with your husband."

"Now, that I do blame you for." She shoved Sandy's hands away from her feet.

"Well, when we met, he…."

"Stop. Don't say another word to me."

"I phoned the police. They should be here soon. I'm so sorry. I really didn't know that you were in here. He said that the trunk was full of his mother's stuff."

"You're lying. I heard you at the gas station. You knew I was in here."

"Then, I did, yeah. But, he told me you wanted to kill me, and that you were violent, and he was just trying to stop you."

"And, you believed him. You left me in here."

"I did believe him until my ex-boyfriend called me. I'm sorry."

Minutes later, the sirens on two police cars drowned out Sandy's and Robin's voices. Four officers rushed out of their cars and over to them.

Robin let the officers help her out of the trunk. Finally, some feeling returned to her legs. She told them that they needed to save the boy that Tim had kidnapped, and she gave them the location to the basement as well as she could remember it.

One of the officers radioed in the information about the basement to Detective Nettle. Another police officer handcuffed Sandy.

Sandy yelled, "I didn't know she was in there."

An officer read Sandy her rights and walked her to one of the squad cars. "Duck. I said duck!" The officer put her hand on top of Sandy's head and guided her toward the back seat.

"I'm telling the truth. I didn't know," Sandy cried. She pushed herself backwards.

Another officer grabbed her. "Save it for the judge. We don't want to hear it."

Robin watched as the two police officers forced Sandy into their patrol car. She was thankful when they drove her away.

The other two officers waited with Robin for an ambulance to arrive. "Medical help will be here soon," one of the officers promised.

"I don't want an ambulance. I just want to see my husband."

The police officers honored her request. They radioed the police helicopter to pick her up and fly her to the same hospital as her husband.

CHAPTER 47

Robin and Tony

Robin's sister waited for her arrival. She hugged her and cried tears of relief with her. "My friend, Dr. Shony is going to examine you and your baby."

"No, I have to see Tony first."

Sharon knew that it would be futile to argue with her. "Oh, all right. Follow me."

Upon entering her husband's room, Robin heard the machines beeping. "What's wrong with him?" she asked, worried.

"Most of his bones are broken." Sharon hugged her lightly. "Robin, he needs a kidney."

"They'll get him one, right?"

"It's not that easy. The surgeon was hoping your brother-in-law would donate a kidney. Your mother-in-law tested negative as a donor. I'm sorry, Robin." She hugged her.

"What about someone else?"

"It would take too long. There'd be too many people ahead of him."

Robin looked at Tony and realized that she was going to lose him. "Could I be alone with him?"

"I'll leave, but I don't think the police officer can."

The young officer, seated in a chair in the corner of the room near the entrance, looked up from his magazine. "I can't."

"He's quiet. You won't even know he's here." Sharon hugged her sister one last time before she left the room.

Robin sat in a chair next to her husband. "Tony, honey, I'm sorry." She waited, but there was no response. "I love you." Now, she cried. "We have a baby on the way. I'll tell him or her about you. I'll make sure that our baby knows you." Tears wet her face. Suddenly, a hand with a tissue appeared beside her. She turned and saw the police officer standing behind her with his arm thrust out at her. "Oh, thank you," she said accepting the tissue.

After he resumed his seat, she began again to talk to her husband. "Tony, I forgive you for that affair, and I want you to forgive me for what I did. I am so sorry. Tony, can you forgive me? Perhaps if we forgive one another, we'll see each other in Heaven." She placed her finger on his one eyebrow and ran her finger lightly across it. This was the only place that she thought it was safe to touch him. It looked like the only place that might not cause him pain.

"Mmmm. Mmmm."

"Tony!" Her hopes rose.

The woman appeared blurry, but she did look familiar. He thought of his wife, Robin. Anytime that he was able to think clearly, meant only one thing: the affects of his medicine had worn off. He tried again to ask for more, but with his jaw wired shut, the best he could do was make sounds that were unintelligible. Tears worked their way out of his one healthy eye. The pain was tremendous.

Robin saw his tears. "Oh, Tony, I'm so glad that you forgive me. Now, we can start a family. The three of us will be so happy."

The buzzer sounded. It beeped loud and long at quick intervals. The police officer looked at her. "Ma-am, you have to push that button: his morphine button. Whenever that machine buzzes, you have to give him more medicine. The nurse has too many patients. I usually do it. It's no big deal really."

Tony made a groaning sound deep inside his throat. He hated being in a state of awareness. The pain was something that if you could sleep through it, and not be around while you were healing, you would rather not be. Push the damn button!

Robin leaned over and kissed his eyebrow. "I'll be right here beside you. I'm going to wait for you to get better. I won't leave here until you do."

Push the damn button. Push the button. Put me out of this pain.

She knew that once she pushed the button, he wouldn't understand her words, and so Robin delayed the action a few more seconds. "Tony," she kissed his eyebrow again and smoothed the fine hair, tracing the line with her finger. "I love you. I never stopped loving you. I will always love you. Our baby will love you, too, because I'll always talk about you. I'll tell him or her how wonderful you were. I promise."

Our what? Ouch! Push the button or kill me, he thought. Please, do one or the other. I don't care which. Please, God, make her do one or the other.

Finally, she pushed the button, and the pain dulled and disappeared. The nice lady finally became quiet. He sank into his happy place and everything was peaceful.

CHAPTER 48

God's Will

It was just after 1:00 a.m., when the detectives located the basement. The information on the egg carton had led them to search a wooded area not far from the park where Tim Henkerson had abducted Jeff Dobbs. The helicopter pilot shined a spotlight on an empty basement that had a dead man's body lying next to it. Officers on the ground discovered two bullet wounds in the victim's chest. They found his driver's license inside his wallet. His name was Gordy Anderson. A bloody shovel was lying next to him, but he did not show any evidence of having been injured from it. This scared the members of the search party, especially Officer John Dobbs.

On the road, police officers had found Tony Henkerson's blue Avenger. Not far from that, they discovered a black pick up.

In the bed of the truck, officers found four, large barrels of toxic chemicals. A fifth one was located in the nearby weeds, next to a freshly dug hole. The registration in the glove box had Gordy Anderson's name on it.

Officer Dobbs found his oldest son's brown, cowboy wallet in the dirt, next to the blue Avenger. Another officer found a pair of tennis shoes. He held them up and asked Officer Dobbs if he recognized them. "Yes, they're Jeff's. Let's go into the woods," he ordered, eager to search for his children.

"No, not yet," Officer Hall called out. "We're waiting for the K-9," he reminded the search party.

There was a trail of blood scattered in drops. It started by the basement and lead into a thick patch of trees and weeds.

Finally, the search was on. With weapons in hands, five officers and three detectives searched the woods. K-9 Officer Cooper sniffed the blood on the shovel that his handler held out to him.

The German Shepard led the search party through the woods and straight to Tim Henkerson who was lying on the ground with John Dobb's 9mm Glock in his right hand. He wasn't dead, but he had lost so much blood through his head injury that his condition was life threatening. Upon further examination, officers and detectives found a bullet wound in his left shoulder. Clearly, this was minor compared to his head wound.

When Detective Nettle gave the pilot orders to fly Tim Henkerson to the hospital, Officer John Dobbs became angry. "No, he can't leave. The chopper is detrimental in this search. The pilot has the greatest view of these woods. We need that searchlight, and what if my sons need emergency transportation?"

Detective Nettle yelled to Officer Dobbs. "The sooner he leaves, the sooner he'll be back."

Dobbs yelled, "My sons better not die and him live."

The chopper left immediately, and everyone resumed the search. One detective found two bullets in the gun that they had recovered from Tim Henkerson. Dobbs reminded everyone that there had only been six bullets. There had been one in Tim, two in the dead man, and two left in his gun. One bullet was still missing.

K-9 Officer Cooper sniffed the brown wallet with the cowboy printed on it. Within minutes, the dog led the team straight to Billy who was lying next to Laura.

Officer Dobbs ran to his son. "Billy." He knelt to the ground and hugged him.

"Ouch! Dad, my arm. I think it's broken. Dad, she's been shot."

One of the other officers felt for a pulse. "We need to get her to a hospital right away." He radioed for the pilot to turn the chopper around.

The pilot's voice sounded through the radio, "I can't. This man might die."

Detective Nettle yelled into his radio, "If Tim Henkerson dies, it will be God's will, but if Laura Knight dies, it will be a tragedy. Turn that damn chopper around and come get her."

"Where's Jeff?" John asked, almost scared to hear the news.

"I don't know," Billy cried. "We all ran in different directions. That way he couldn't shoot all of us. This lady," he still had his healthy arm near her and his hand in hers, "pushed us in front of her and told us to run. She knew he was going to shoot her. She tried to save us. I guess I ran in a circle, 'cause I came right back to her. I wrapped my shirt around her and tied a knot over her wound just like they taught us in boy scouts."

"Good job, Son." He gently patted his head, resisting the urge to hug him, so as not to hurt his arm again.

"That man wants to kill us, Dad," he said sounding scared.

"Son, he's been caught."

"I shot him, Dad. I used your gun." He stood up.

"Billy, why didn't you come to me? Why didn't you tell me what was going on?"

Billy began crying. "It was my fault, Dad. I took that phone, and he took Jeff. It was my fault." Tears were streaming down his cheeks.

"John lightly hugged him, trying not to hurt his injured arm. "It's okay, Son." He cried, too.

The medics carried Laura onto the helicopter and placed her next to Tim Henkerson. Just as they did, Mary Dobbs arrived. She saw her husband and Billy and ran to them.

"Be careful with his arm," John warned, but it was too late. His wife already had Billy in a tight embrace, drenching him in tears of joy.

"Mom, my arm!"

She backed up. "John, he's hurt."

"Ride in the ambulance with him to the hospital," he told his wife as he gave her a hug.

"Where's Jeff?" she asked worried.

John was teary eyed when he spoke. "We haven't found him yet."

She broke down crying. He hugged her again. "Honey, be strong for Billy."

Mary blotted her face with the sleeves of her shirt. Taylor ran to them. "Billy," she yelled and began to hug him. The warning about his arm was once again too late in coming.

His sister joined him and their mother in the ambulance. She, too, was distraught over the news that Jeff was still missing, but like her mother, she was trying to be brave for Billy.

The dog was ready to track again. His handler held one of Jeff's shoes under K-9 Officer Cooper's nose. The dog took deep sniffs and ran through the woods leading the search party on a chase that lasted almost a mile. Officer Cooper located Jeff and sat next to him. He barked until his handler and the other officers caught up to him.

Jeff had been on the ground, huddled into a ball, asleep. He woke up to the dog's barks, and he knew that his father had found him. He petted the dog.

"Jeff," John cried.

His son ran to him. "Daddy, I knew you would come. I knew you'd find me," he cried happily. "Did you find Billy?"

"Yes, we found him."

"The bad guy hurt Billy's arm."

"He's going to be all right. Mom's with him at the hospital," he cried, unable to hold back any tears. His youngest son was in one piece, and he was safe. John hugged him tightly.

"The bad guy shot that lady. Is she dead?"

"No. She's at the hospital, too."

"Billy shot the bad guy, but he didn't die."

"We caught the bad guy. You're safe now." He hugged his son again.

"That bad guy shot a man who tried to save us. Is he dead?"

"Yes, son, that man died."

John carried his son out of the woods and placed him in his patrol car. He and his partner drove to the hospital to be with the rest of the family.

CHAPTER 49

Family

Anne Knight received a much-awaited phone call. "Thank God," She cried with joy, and then she gasped.

Jill and Danny read her face. They knew it was a mixture of good and bad news. Once she was off the phone, she informed them that the search team had found Laura, but she needed surgery. Tim Henkerson had shot her.

Without hesitation, they hurried into Danny's car, and he drove them to the hospital. They were not the only people worried about a loved one in the hospital. The Dobbs family waited in the recovery room for their son who was having a pin implanted into his broken arm. The Andersons were at the hospital to identify their son who was in the morgue in the basement. Then, there was the Henkerson family. Tony was about to die, and Tim had already been pronounced brain dead.

Lilly Henkerson was beside herself as to what she should do. Perhaps someone who had not been Tim's mother could have made the decision much quicker. She was suffering an emotional crisis about signing a paper that would kill one son, so that the other could live.

Robin was holding Tony's hand when Lilly walked into his room. "I signed it," she said. "The nurse is going to take Tim off life support. I couldn't watch," she cried.

Robin stepped away from Tony and hugged Lilly. She didn't know what to say to her, so she stayed silent.

Tony still had absolutely no comprehension of what was taking place. It would be at least a week before he would be clearheaded and off his haze-inducing drugs. That's when he would learn that his brother was removed from life support so that he could live.

Two orderlies entered Tony's room. One of them said, "We need to get him prepped."

Robin and Lilly both said their good-byes to Tony. Robin lightly kissed one of his eyebrows. Then the two Henkerson women walked to the visitors' room.

Family members of the victims, the heroes, and the perpetrators shared one large room. It was uncomfortably quiet until Jeff Dobbs started telling his sister everything that had happened to him. "We were playing with that cell phone that Billy took from Dad, and the bad guy wanted to buy it from us. He looked mean, so we didn't give it to him. I tried to run away, but he caught me. He tied me up and hit me. The lady, Robin, was nice. He hit her, too. He tied her up, and he took her away. Hey, there you are," he said having spotted her in the room. Jeff smiled at her.

Robin walked over to him, bent down by his chair, and gave him a hug. "I'm glad you're safe." Then she left the room with her mother-in-law, who could not handle hearing the horrible things that her son, Tim, had done.

Jeff continued his story. "Then Billy came. I could hear his voice. He tried to save me, but he got tied up, too. Then the cat came and that lady. I don't know what happened to the cat. I could hear it running around, and that man was chasing it. That lady took a picture of me on her cell phone, and the bad guy tied her up, too. Then he untied us and made us walk to the parking lot. He kept pointing a gun at me. He made us throw some boxes away and get into a blue car. We went to the car wash, and he tied us up again. Then he took us to the woods and tried to kill us. When he was going to throw me into the basement, Billy got his hands and feet untied. The bad guy had me up in the air, and that's when Billy took Dad's gun out of the bad guy's pocket and shot him. The bad guy threw me on the ground and broke Billy's arm. He took the gun away from Billy. He was going to shoot him, but a man came out of nowhere and hit the bad guy in the head with a shovel. The bad guy shot him twice."

This is when the Andersons, Gordy's mother and father, began crying. Their son was a hero. Even though the police informed them that he had been illegally dumping toxic chemicals, they were still proud of him. Gordy had given his life to save a child.

"Then the bad guy chased after us. That lady pushed Billy and me in front of her, and the bad guy shot her in the back. I heard her scream, but I kept running like she told me to."

Now, Laura's mother cried. Her daughter had a bullet in her back. If something went wrong during surgery, she could be paralyzed or die.

"Billy and I just kept running. I didn't want to run in the dark by myself, but Billy yelled at me. He said that if we stayed together, we would both get shot. I was scared, but I did what Billy said, and I ran a long time, too." Then his voice became excited. "Then Daddy found me."

Taylor hugged her brother. "I'm so glad he found you."

"Did you miss me? I missed you. I kept thinking about the times you let me play with your Guitar Hero, and when you tickled me, and when you made me mac n cheese."

"Yes, I missed you." She tickled him, and he laughed.

Epilogue

❀

Almost five months later, Laura, Jill, and Danny met in Robin Henkerson's hospital room to see the new additions to the family. Little Jill and Jenny Henkerson were healthy, sweet, and adorable, identical twins. Tony was still recovering from some of his many injuries. He carefully held one baby, and Robin held the other.

Jill looked at the proud parents and then at Danny. "That will be us soon."

"Give me a year to adjust to our marriage first," Danny commented.

Jill looked disappointed. "You're not adjusted yet?"

Officer Mark Hall arrived and brought matching pink balloons with the words Baby Girl written on them. He kissed Laura and stood beside her.

Jill smiled proudly at the two of them. She had told Laura several times that if she had not involved herself in the next-door neighbors' lives, then Mark and she would not have met, fallen in love, and become engaged.

Laura had been lucky. The bullet missed her spine and other vital organs. Her surgery and recovery were both excellent. Other than a few scars, she didn't have any long lasting medical problems from being shot that night.

While she had been healing in the hospital, Mark Hall visited her almost daily and brought her flowers and her favorite dessert: brownies. By the time she recovered, they had fallen in love.

Fred wheeled Edna into the room. "We've come to see the babies."

"What did the doctor say?" Laura asked Fred. She knew today was a big day for them as well.

"He said that Edna's cancer is in remission."

"Oh, that's wonderful!" Laura said excited.

Everyone made congratulatory comments to the Greenways for their good news. They likewise made many compliments to the Henkersons on their beautiful daughters.

The hospital room was full of happy people celebrating life. The door opened and John Dobbs and his family entered. His wife was carrying a large bouquet of colorful flowers. Jeff and Billy were excited to see the tiny babies. Tony handed baby Jenny to Taylor. She held the baby carefully while her brother, Jeff, touched the baby's tiny fingers.

Fred walked over to Billy. "How are you doing?"

"My arm's all better now."

Mary Dobbs smiled at Fred. "He's doing fine. They both are."

Sharon entered the room with her son. She walked over to Robin, "Sis, how are you doing?"

"I'm great. Thanks for the private room."

"I pulled a few strings, but what are sisters for?"

Craig saw Taylor and smiled. He crossed over to her like a magnet. "Aren't my cousins cute?"

Taylor smiled back. "Are you going to baby-sit?"

"If someone offers to help me, I will." Craig swung his head back, slinging his hair to one side so that he could see her with two eyes. He pulled up his pants and smiled.

Taylor's father stepped in between them. "Here, Taylor, let me hold the baby. You go over there and help your mother put the flowers in a vase."

Tony's mother entered. "Where are my grandbabies?" She took baby Jenny from John Dobbs. "Oh, Tony, I'm so happy that you named her Jenny after my mother."

Robin handed her other baby daughter to Jill. "You know why I named her after you?"

Jill smiled. She touched the tiny baby's soft cheek.

"I named my first-born after you because you were constantly looking out for my safety. I don't think anyone could ask for a better neighbor."

Jill smiled. "Thank you. Say, that reminds me. I want to invite all of you to our block party. It doesn't matter if you don't live on our block. It will be fun. Danny hired a band and everything. We are going to have tons of food and drinks. And, there will be dancing in the streets."

"Are you trying to show off your home now that it's remodeled?" Laura asked jokingly.

Jill looked at her seriously. "No, I'm just making an effort to get to know my neighbors."

Author Biography

Kelly Phillips is the author of the mystery, *Justified Conspiracy*. She's a graduate of the University of Michigan and teaches language arts. She resides in Romulus, Michigan with her husband, Mark. They are currently working on screenplays and a collection of short stories.